Sparks

Ahmed A. Khan

Golden Acorn Press

Cover Art © 2008 Seth Crossman

A Golden Acorn Press Book
384 Markowitz Road
Parish, NY 13131

Copyright © 2008 by Ahmed A. Khan
ISBN 978-0-9801921-2-4
First Edition November 2008

Printed in the United States of America

Copyright Acknowledgements

Contents

xi Introduction

11 The Meaning of Life and Other Cliches

18 A Peace of Sorts

24 Face It

28 Fault

37 Love and Life

41 Point Counter Point

45 Synchronicity

61 T. Gips and the Time Flies

65 The Book of Pain

71 Wordspell

91 The Maker Myth

95 Traveler From an Antique Land

101 The Presonic Man

104 Tug of War

118 Angels

"One who knows oneself knows God." Ali ibn Abi Talib

Introduction

For a moment I want to talk about food. It is something I love to experience, not only by making forays into my kitchen and tasting the effect every spice in my cabinet has on the food I cook, but also by going out to dinner at good restaurants. I have found that a good restaurant is a night's satisfaction in itself. Perhaps I am a glutton, or perhaps, I just feel it is worth enjoying something I do three times a day, every day of my life.

On normal nights, I sit down to the table and have dinner. If I am lucky, I might have a salad before hand and dessert after. It is only on the special occasions that I go out to dinner and run the gambit, even tackling a tasty appetizer in addition to my salad, my dinner, and my dessert.

At good French restaurants, or with an authentic French experience, eating is taken to another level. Everything put onto the table is chosen for looks and for taste, including the drink selection. A good French cook makes his choices for a reason. He may serve a fruit salad first because it has light, fresh, and crisp tastes that refresh the palette. With it comes a soft bubbly champagne. Together, the salad and bubbly champagne leave the diner wanting more. Dinner may be small samplings of seasoned vegetables and small pieces of steak smothered in a heavy, strong sauce. With it comes a more full bodied wine that brings out the taste of the meat. When dessert comes, it will often be sweet and sugary, something that leaves the diner with a good taste in the mouth long after the meal has ended. Each choice served its purpose. Each choice brought something different to the meal.

This collection of stories by Ahmed A. Khan is a writer's French dinner.

Ahmed A. Khan writes with the same kind of attention a French cook displays in his cooking. Each story in this collection tastes different and each has been chosen on purpose. Like a good chef, Ahmed has a wide range of stories, from pure entertainment to serious thinkers, that can appeal to many different tastes. "T. Gips and the Time Flies" is light and whimsical with a main character that is hard to take seriously. Ahmed gets deep and philosophical with "The Meaning of Life and Other Cliches" and "Synchronicity." He breathes life and emotional intensity into his characters in "A Peace of Sorts" and "Angels." Ahmed displays his ability to stretch conventional story parameters with "Love and Life" and "Point Counter Point." And perhaps some of his most impressive stories may be those that hinge on a single provocative idea like in "The Maker Myth" and "The Presonic Man."

Ahmed A. Khan certainly has shown himself to be a unique and talented writer, offering up a collection of stories that will be an experience for any reader.

—Seth Crossman

The Meaning of Life and Other Cliches

This story was first published in 2005 at Anotherealm where it went on to win the Higney Award for best story that year. Later, it won an honorable mention in the Parallax Awards.

Once, I traveled to a remote place where I knew no one. The feeling of loneliness was quite intense and it made me think. This story is the result of those musings and took me six years to write.

1

Half past one, GMT, earthwise.

The kids would have come home from school now.

She would be having her lunch.

What the hell!

What's wrong?

How long are we going to be earthbound? When are we going to re-
alize that we are stranded—trapped—on this planet of tall mountains,
huge lakes and thick jungles and no sentient life? We will be spending
the rest of our lives here, both of us.

I still don't get it. What's wrong with thinking and talking about
earth and—and about our people back there?

But damn it! It seems so useless, so futile.

So do a lot of other things, like us sitting here and tossing pebbles
into the lake.

One of these days, I think I am going to toss my watch into the
lake. It doesn't seem right, counting the days and nights of this planet
in earthly units of time.

Hmm. You are right. It does seem out of place. Don't worry about
your watch, though. One of these days its battery is going to run down
and it will stop functioning and you will be saved from the bother of
throwing it into the lake.

2

Do you see those strange, creatures floating on the air?

Remind me of manta rays.

Remind me more of the mythical will-o-the-wisps.

Are they predators? Could they harm us?

Why take chances? Let us hide in the cave.

3

Are you afraid of loneliness?

Yes, yes I am.

So am I.

Why?

Why what?

Why do we fear loneliness?

I have a pet theory about it. When I am lonely—with no ties of companionship with anybody—then my mind starts working in a strange way. It projects the immenseness of the multidimensional cosmos before me and against this background I find myself, my whole existence, too small, too insignificant, too unimportant. And it is this feeling of insignificance that a person fears.

And what happens when a person is not alone?

Then links and bonds are formed between that person and the companions. With these links and bonds comes strength. With these links and bonds, the existence of the person spreads itself beyond the person remaining insignificant no longer.

4

I dreamt of her today.

I too dreamt of my wife and children.

Did your wife and children speak to you in your dream?

As a matter of fact, they did.

She spoke to me today.

What did she say?

She said she loves me, and she smiled and there were tears in her eyes. Did I ever tell you that she gets dimples when she smiles? We were planning to get married this year.

Of what use are dreams?

Dreams are real. They are just a different kind of reality.

Listen. I just had a dreadful thought. What would happen if back there on earth, your girlfriend, my wife and kids, our friends, in short all the people who love us all of a sudden stopped loving us, stopped thinking about us, stopped caring for us?

Shut up.

Huh?

Don't say it. Don't even think it. It should not happen. It cannot happen. I will always be remembered.

Yes. I can see you feel about it the same way that I do. But why? In God's name, why? Why do we feel the way we do? Of what importance to us are thoughts and feelings of people billions of miles away from us? Can you answer me that? Can you?

No. The only thing I know is that this belief that someone somewhere really loves me, this belief is one of those very few things on the basis of which I can say that not all of my life had been a waste.

Yes. Put that way, love seems to be the prime function—or one of the prime functions—of life, doesn't it?

To love and be loved.

To love and be loved.

5

Those will-o-the-wisps seem harmless.

They seem to like sticking around with us.

And don't they look beautiful, dancing on the air?

Do you think they are sentient?

I hope so.

Somehow, it seems important, doesn't it?

6

Let us forget the woes and count the blessings.

Okay. To begin with, we are alive. We didn't die in the spaceship crash. We were not even hurt much.

This planet is livable.

We have found a nice and cozy cave to live in.

Our stores of food will last us for months and by then we should be able to find edible fruits and such on this planet.

We have each other for company.

And probably a good thing that one of us is not a woman. This way we avoid the complications of being the new Adam and Eve for this planet.

And the planet, on the surface, is not a bad looking one. It has some beautiful scenery.

And the books. Don't forget the books we managed to salvage from the wreck. We have the Bible, the Qur'an, and those poetry collections —Keats, Tennyson, Elliot.

And we have the sense of wonder, the desire for knowledge, and this planet might—just might—prove interesting.

7

I have noticed something. I dream more often and more intensely when the will-o-the-wisps are near me.

Strange. Now that you put it into words, of late my dreams seem more and more real to me.

Reminds me of a line I read somewhere: What are dreams if not a different kind of reality?

8

It is strange, isn't it, the way our perspective changes with time? Things always seem different when you look at them in retrospect.

Yes. The sense of values changes. What seemed important then seems trivial now. That which was trivial then appears important now. These days I never even think about who is going to win the next elections back home, but I do often think of the way my mother used to kiss me goodbye every morning when I left for school so many years ago.

There is another thing. In retrospect, I have nothing more than a vague memory of the hurts I received in life. Even when put together and taken collectively, these hurts don't seem to amount to much. But when I think of all the hurts that I have dished out to others—

I know what you are talking about. Regrets. A whole lot of regrets. That day when I slapped my kid when all he did was ask me to buy him a chocolate ice cream.

That day when my mother asked me to get her a book from the library and I refused saying that I couldn't leave my favorite TV program.

How many times have I hurt my wife unreasonably, pigheadedly, just out to prove that I was the boss of the house.

How many times did I simply neglect—and sometimes even crush —the feelings of others.

And they—all of them—were people who loved us.

Loved us and cared for us and—

And we—

Regrets. And pain. And a soul screaming for a second chance.

You are crying!

Do you mind? No, you would not. You are crying too.

Yes. Let us cry ourselves to sleep.

9

Life seems so meaningless now.

Do you think the will-o-the-wisps are sentient?

A strange response to my observation about the meaning of life.

I somehow feel that our life will be meaningful again if the will-o-the-wisps are sentient.

What is the meaning of life?

I don't know. Do you?

10

Most of our problems back on earth—they seem so petty now.

So many of concerns misplaced.

So many actions futile.

Now we learn.

11

Other than home and family and friends, what are the things you miss the most?

Why do you always have to ask these painful questions? Why can't you leave memories well enough alone?

Catharsis man, catharsis.

Catharsis my foot. I think the concept of catharsis is humbug. Another blunder of modern psychology.

Okay, then let us talk about these things to pass our time.

Alright then. I will join you. I miss the little things—those things that many good writers wrote about in their books.

Things like?

The stone benches in the park.

The early morning strollers.

The dim, dark streets of the night.

The children going to and coming back from school.

The tea house and the steam rising up from the tea cups.

The town library with its dimly lit corners where the mysterious smell of old books hung in the air, like the smell of captured time.

The birds.

And the bees.

Ha, ha!

12

Say, my watch has stopped. What about yours?

Hmm? Mine seems to have stopped too. The batteries have run down at last.

So shall we toss them into the lake now?

Again, why bother? Why not just take them off and leave them lying around on this rock?

Yeah. Why not?

And I do believe the will-o-the-wisps are sentient creatures. Let us see if we can communicate with them.

A Peace of Sorts

A never before published hard SF/mystical story set on the moon.

The relaxation exercises are not working. Neither is meditation. It is 2 AM, moon standard time and I am tense and jittery as I sit on my bed in a room in Lunatel, the unimaginatively named hotel on the moon.

My room is small. It is on the top floor, and does not have any windows. Instead, it has a huge glass roof that provides a breathtaking view of the skies once I shut off all the artificial lights in the room. A meteor shower has been predicted. I look up, hoping to see it, but remember quickly that this will not be possible. The moon has no atmosphere to burn the meteors and create a display.

I try to lose myself in the moon night but I cannot obliterate a vision that I keep seeing without the use of my eyes—the face of my wife, serene and beautiful even in death, serene and beautiful in spite of the marks of violence.

I ring up the room service.

"Could you send up two glasses of warm milk?" Milk is expensive on the moon, but I can afford it.

"Certainly, Mr. Ali." There is no evidence of surprise. By now, they know some of my ways.

Within five minutes, the doorbell rings.

"Lights on," I say. The roof becomes opaque and the lights slowly come on.

"Brighter", and the lights grow perceptibly brighter.

"Come in."

The waiter enters and deposits the glasses of milk on the center table. I look at the waiter. He appears to be Asian, probably in his late fifties or early sixties, close to retirement age. His face is lined and his eyes are empty. His name tag reads: Ram Prasad. Probably a fellow country man. He is about to leave but I want to try not to be alone as long as possible.

"Please have a seat, Ram Prasad," I point to the couch. "I would like to talk to you."

His eyes show surprise. He sits down but his manner is awkward, wary.

"From India?"

He nods.

"So am I."

He smiles, the barriers coming down a few notches. I pick up one glass of milk and offer him the other. He protests. I smile and over-ride his protests. He sips his milk. Suddenly, I see tears in his eyes.

"Are you okay?" I say, alarmed.

He bows his head and nods. "I guess I had forgotten how it feels to be treated as a human being."

I let him alone for some time. Then I break the silence. "I have seen how badly the manager, Mr. Haysfire, treats you. Why do you stay?"

"Because I am a waiter and I cannot be anything else, and this is the only hotel on the moon."

"Why not go back to India?"

"My wife and my daughter are buried here, on the moon. I cannot leave them alone."

I wonder at how lives interweave. Here is another tie between this person and me.

"Mr. Haysfire is a racist, isn't he?" I say.

"The worst kind." His eyes express disgust. "If this was earth and the last century, he would be a KKK leader."

"A person who would think nothing of raping and killing a non-white woman." Something in my voice touches him. He looks up at me. Abruptly, he gets up. "I have to go, sir." He leaves the room, leaving me alone with my thoughts.

I step out of my room. The door clicks shut behind me. I step on the conveyor belt going right. Two rooms down, the corridor turns left. Two more rooms and I step off the conveyor belt and knock on the door in front of me.

"Come in."

Colonel Nordstrad is a giant—a giant in a wheelchair. Ex-army, turned private investigator after retirement.

"Here's my report." He hands me a folder. Given his appearance, his voice is surprisingly soft.

Ahmed A. Khan

"You have conclusive proof?" My heart is beating fast.

"Conclusive enough for you and me, but nothing that will hold up in a court. Sorry."

Back in my room, I study the report. I finish reading it. Then I spread my pray mat and pray.

Nordstrad is right. The evidence is conclusive for him and me. One day, ten years ago, while staying at this hotel, I had gone moon-walking. Upon my return, I had found my wife brutally raped and murdered in our room. She had not been able to make any noise because her mouth had been taped. Subsequent investigation had resulted in no arrests. The perpetrator had not been found. I had been harboring my suspicions—suspicions to which I could now attach a name: Haysfire.

The ball is now in my court.

Ram Prasad. Ram Prasad is my key to the next step.

Haysfire sleeps alone in his apartment. He does not have a family. People like Haysfire usually do not have families. Thank God. When he is rudely shaken awake, he tries to sit up, but he cannot. He has been securely tied to his bed. He cannot even make a noise because his mouth has been taped shut.

He looks at me and there is fear in his eyes. He looks at the knife in my gloved hand.

"You remember me, don't you?" I say. "And my wife, Firdaus."

He tries to move and makes vague noises.

"For ten years, a sense of injustice has been burning through my soul. Time to balance the scales of justice."

I move toward him. He is not moving any longer, as if he has given up every hope. Only his eyes move, and there is stark terror in them. Suddenly I sense a stench that starts slowly but grows strong. I recognize it. Haysfire has lost control of his bladder.

I raise the knife, pause, and move back in disgust. I cannot do it. I cannot kill someone in cold blood. I move away from the bed, put the knife back in the kitchen where I had taken it from, and leave his apartment.

I take the elevator down to the main floor. The lobby is cozy and beautifully lit. The girl at the reception desk smiles at me.

"I want to go out," I say. She calls for the concierge who brings me a space suit. I don it and move to the exit. The door opens and I step into the air lock. The door closes behind me and another door opens in front of me and I am out in the open. The deep, dark airlessness of moonspace. The silent, ghostly buildings of the settlement.

Old scenarios of moon colonies had depicted air tight domes. But in reality they proved unfeasible. What we have instead are individually air-tight buildings with air locks. Many of these buildings are connected to each other through underground tunnels.

The silence of the moon night calms me. The vast, overwhelming sky full of stars shows me the insignificance of my affairs and my existence. I remember the predicted meteor showers. The meteors may be on their way. Some of them may even hit the moon surface, though this is an extremely rare occurrence. It might be safer for me to go back inside.

But before I go, I raise my hands to the sky and pray. Then I make my way back to the hotel. I know that I will be arrested for assault and breaking and entering because Haysfire is sure to put the police on to me once he manages to remove the ropes and the gag.

I enter the hotel, a repair crew is busy working. It seems a small meteorite had managed to penetrate one of the hotel rooms, depressurizing it. Before I can find out what room was hit I am arrested for suspicion of murder.

Later, they let me go. The room that was hit by the meteorite was Haysfire's. They found the pebble-sized meteorite embedded in his head where it had hit him and killed him. A very strange turn of events. Also, it is proved beyond doubt that I was not in the hotel when Haysfire died. I was outside. The ropes and gag did indicate some sort of foul play but they do not have enough evidence to pin it on me.

Before going back to my room, I confront Police Chief Gardner.

"You have to admit that suspicion of murder was justified under the circumstance," the Police Chief said. "The rope, the gag..."

"But why is it that among the fifty or so people in the hotel I was the only person arrested on suspicion? No one else in the hotel was even investigated, as far as I know."

"Because... because..."

"Is it because I am a Muslim and the stereotypes created ages ago back on earth are still clinging to our psyches?"

Ahmed A. Khan

The Police Chief had the grace to look sheepish.

More than a century ago, A.C. Clarke, a writer, had hoped that we would not take our baggage—our borders, our prejudices—to space. But I guess that was hoping for too much.

Back in my room, I analyze my feelings and find that there is a peace of sorts in my heart and mind. In a way, I think I have avenged my wife.

Underneath the starry skies of the moon, I had prayed—prayed hard—for Haysfire's death.

Face It

Physiognomy suggests that the character traits of a person can be deduced by studying the facial features. So how does this relationship work? If a character trait of a person changes, will it trigger a change in a facial feature? Alternatively, if a facial feature changes, will it trigger a change in the character? Interesting questions, no?

The automobile accident disfigured my face.

"I could give you a brand new face," my friend Dr. James Mannering offered. Jim was the top plastic surgeon in town.

I am a complacent guy by nature. "I don't care much about my face," I informed him. "Inside, I am still me."

Jim shrugged. "You are still young. You may need your pretty face one of these days, at least to please your wife."

"Jenna loves me and not my pretty face," I replied.

I was wrong. Jenna left me.

So here I was, in Jim's office, asking him to give me back my pretty face after all.

Jim looked at me thoughtfully.

"What yuh staring at, bub?" I did an adequate impression of a famous comic book character. That is one of the ways I react to stress. I start fooling around.

"I have a theory that I would like to test on you—with your permission, of course."

"Making me a guinea pig?"

"It won't harm you in any way. I guarantee."

"Explain," I said.

"Are you a good judge of character?"

"I have to be, in my position as the recruitment officer of my corporation."

"Can you tell if a person is intelligent, honest and friendly just by looking at the face?"

"In many cases, yes."

"How?"

That made me think. I thought and I thought but could not come up with a specific answer. So finally, I shrugged and said, "I don't know."

"I have done a bit of research and it is my opinion that certain facial characteristics are interrelated to some inherent character traits."

"So?"

"So what if we modify a facial feature? Would it lead to a modification of a character trait?"

I was intrigued. "What do you want to do with me?"

"What I would like is to make your face an exact replica of the face of another person and see if your character traits change to reflect the personality of the model."

That gave me pause.

"Interesting idea," I said at last.

"So who would you like to be?"

I picked up a piece of scrap paper, pulled out my pen and started doodling on it. I tend to do it automatically when I am in deep thought.

"Let's see," I mused. "I always wanted to be a writer. Can you think of a good writer? Someone who was popular, intelligent and of good disposition. Oh, and of course he should not be bad to look at."

"Wow! When go out you go all out, don't you? Anything else?"

"I think it would avoid a lot of confusion if that writer also happened to be dead."

"Good thinking. Now let us look at some possibilities."

For the next quarter of an hour we bandied names.

"Shakespeare?" he suggested.

"No. All we have about his appearance are artists' representations. Who knows how accurate these are."

"Byron?"

"I said a writer not a poet."

"Shaw?"

"Good looking?"

"Hemingway?"

"Suicidal."

Suddenly Jim snapped his fingers. "I have just the person. Asimov."

"The famous science fiction writer? I've heard about him but never read any of his books. I am not into SF, you know."

"So what do you think?"

"Hmm! Do you have his picture around?"

"Let me see if I can find a picture of him on the Net."

It did not take long. Soon, I was looking at the face of Isaac Asimov on the computer screen. The guy was quite good looking.

"I guess he was in his twenties when this photo was taken," Jim commented.

"Okay, then make me look twentyish once again. I don't mind looking ten years younger than I am now."

The operation was a success.

I resumed my normal life. Jim called almost everyday to find out if I found any changes in my personality, my likes and dislikes. As a matter of fact, even I was curious to know if I would change into something that I was not.

One day, hardly a couple of weeks after the change of face, I felt an irresistible urge to write. Jim's theory seemed to be working.

I sat down at my computer, and started my word processor application. While I looked at the blank page on the screen, strange and wonderful ideas seemed to invade my mind. My hands flew on the keyboard. Words seemed to flow smoothly, effortlessly—from my brain, through my fingertips on the keyboard to the computer screen. Very soon, I had a complete story.

I felt drained and elated at the same time—the way one feels after a session of great lovemaking. I went back to the beginning and re-read the story I had just written. My elation increased as I read on. It was a beautiful story—highly interesting, well-crafted, and it put forward a unique concept. I was sure that I had written a masterpiece. I was now a writer, just as good as Asimov.

The story was about a planet with multiple suns where night fell only once in several hundred years. And "Nightfall" was a perfect name for it.

Fault

A comic book creator sent me a sketch for a comic book character called "Earthangel" and asked for a script. I sent in the script for a 20-pager within a week, but the comic series went defunct. In addition to a comic book type hero, this story has aliens and geology and a fly swatter.

The story appears here for the first time.

The President looked at the aerial photograph lying on the table before him. It showed an alien spacecraft in a desert. Dead bodies and broken weapons lay scattered around it.

Almost absentmindedly, he pressed a button on the side of his table. A screen to his right lighted up and showed the visage of the Internal Security Chief of Staff.

"Report," ordered the President.

"Bad news, sir. Our mission is facing some unexpected challenges."

"I can see as much. I have the photo before me. Tell me what happened."

The Chief cleared his throat. "The nukes just didn't go off. The aliens seem to have the power to blanket out all nuclear reactions."

The President bent forward and to the right, putting his face close to the screen.

"Do you know what this means?"

"Yes," said the Chief. "This means that the aliens were not making idle threats. They can totally destroy us if they want. All they have to do is blanket the nuclear reactions within the sun, as they said they would do if we do not offer total surrender."

"Do you have any suggestions now?"

"Sir, I was thinking… Why don't we put Project Earthknight to use?"

The President's face lit-up and a tight smile appeared on his lips.

"Yeah. Great idea," he said eagerly. "Send the tin can against them. Either he will beat the aliens off or we will be rid of the armored idiot. Either way, we win."

"We did choose the wrong guy for the project, didn't we?" the Chief said ruefully.

The President slammed the tabletop with his fist.

"Who could have thought that the son of an ex-officer of IS would turn out to be a god damn do-gooder ready to go against us—his creators—over what he calls his principles?"

"And the publicity we gave him didn't do any good either. He has become the people's favorite. Any overt action against him and you could say goodbye to your re-election."

"You telling me? I know it. I know it. But perhaps this is our chance. Let the aliens take care of him."

Early the next morning, while it was just getting light, the IS air car reached the house of Gary Vanguard. It was an old house, rambling and quaint. He had inherited it from his parents.

The air car, after picking up Gary, lifted off the ground and sped away.

Gary quickly dressed up in his Earthknight armor, except for his helmet.

"Hey Moe! What's it this time?" the tall young man addressed the pilot.

"Call me Moe just once more and I will kill you," said the woman.

"Okay, okay, Morgana, then. Now tell me what is going on."

"Aliens, of course," responded Morgana.

"Aliens? But there was nothing in the news."

"No, there wasn't," said Morgana. "Strange thing is that the aliens seem to want to avoid publicity too. They landed their spaceship in a remote, uninhabited spot. They radioed in an ultimatum demanding our unconditional surrender. And they did it using modulated frequency signals that could be received only on our equipment."

"Ultimatum demanding surrender? What did the ultimatum say?"

"Surrender unconditionally or we will destroy your sun."

Gary's face registered a mild shock. "Whoosh!" he said.

Morgana smiled. "As per tradition, the correct expression in these circumstances is 'sheesh'!" she said.

"But why us?" Gary asked. "Why not some other country?"

"Today America, tomorrow the world," said Morgana nonchalantly.

"Where's the spaceship supposed to be?"

"Near San Andreas."

"Now why does that name ring a bell?"

"Could it be because it is a well-known place in America?"

Ahmed A. Khan

"Yeah! I got it now," Gary said, ignoring Morgana's comment. "There was an earthquake in that region last week. Was it caused by the ship landing?"

"No. The ship landed two days after the quake," said Morgana.

Gary put on his helmet. The helmet covered his face, changing it into a black, featureless oval. It was the only non-metallic part of the suit, and was made of bullet-proof plastic. Fully dressed, he looked like a black tin giant. The suit was smooth and displayed graceful curves, except for the varied weaponry distributed all over it and the back jets that gave it the ability to fly. It was strong and much lighter than it looked.

"So what's the situation now?" asked Earthknight.

"The aliens challenged us to attack them," Morgana said. "Our troops did. With nukes. And failed!"

Earthknight sat down on the large seat specially provided to accommodate his armor. "The nukes failed. And they are sending ME to face these aliens? What am I supposed to do?"

"The chief has an idea," Morgana said. "You are to be taken prisoner by the aliens. Then you are supposed to destroy the ship from the inside, where it may not be that invulnerable."

"How does the chief come up with these great ideas?"

"Look, there's the spaceship," Morgana pointed to the view panel. The air car was hovering over the alien spacecraft. It was huge.

Earthknight moved towards the door of the air car. "And what will you be doing while I risk my butt down there?"

"I will be hovering above, observing your progress." Morgana smiled sweetly.

Earthknight opened the door and jumped out. He smiled as he activated the armor jets and slowly floated down.

He landed near the alien ship and looked at the corpses spread around it.

"Don't these sons of bitches from space have anything better to do than come and try to conquer earth?" he said to the wind.

He sat down near a corpse.

"Who are you guys?" He asked the dead. "What are you doing here? What purpose did your deaths serve in the grand design?"

The helmet hid his face and his tears as well.

"Do you have any relatives? Wife, parents, brothers, sisters, children? What kind of a family do you come from? Did you have good parents? Were you a good son to them?"

He lifted up the head of the corpse and looked carefully into the face. It seemed to be the face of a young man.

"What was your purpose in life? Did you fulfil your purpose?"

The corpse didn't answer. The dead rarely do.

Gary stood up. Enough of waxing philosophical, Gary dear, he admonished himself. Get along with your job.

He turned to the ship and attacked the hull with his laser. Minutes later, he shut the laser down.

"Didn't even smudge the paint job on that hull," he murmured. "Now all I have to do is wait for the welcoming committee to come out and capture me."

He waited.

"Will they capture me?"

He waited.

"Or kill me?"

He waited.

"Come on, get me." He gave the hull a kick.

An opening appeared on the top of the hull and something like a gigantic fly swatter emerged out of it.

The gigantic fly swatter swatted Earthknight and swished back inside the spaceship.

"Now what am I supposed to do?" thought Gary while he lay face down on the ground. "The damned aliens seem to have a sense of humor which is almost human."

He got up and reactivated his jets. Once again he was hovering over the spaceship, wondering what to do next. The air car buzzed around him like an irritating fly.

He then saw something far off. It seemed to be some sort of a construction—a big structure in the middle of nowhere. Curious, he extended the armor's telescopic sight. He could just make out the huge board over the gate. It read: SAN ANDREAS SEISMIC RESEARCH STATION. A few cars and trucks were parked in front of the gate.

San Andreas. Seismic research. The association of ideas brought back memories of his graduate years and his geology lessons. A worm of an idea burrowed its way up his subconscious. He flew towards the research station and landed just outside the gate.

Ahmed A. Khan

The air car landed behind him. The door of the air car opened and Morgana stepped out.

"The fly swatter," she said and started laughing uncontrollably.

Earthknight glared at her, but of course she could not see the glare behind his helmet.

They entered the gate.

Eventually, they found themselves sitting in an office. It was clean, sparsely furnished with a table and a few chairs. On one side of the table, face forward, sat a slightly plump, bespectacled, middle aged lady, who must have been quite attractive a decade or so ago. A plaque on the table proclaimed her to be Dr. Susan Reickert, Assistant Director. There was a window behind her, but it was closed and the blinds had been pulled down. The only illumination was from an overhead light.

Dr. Reickert spoke. "Normally, I don't see people at this time of the day, but it seems that a suit such as yours can do wonders when it comes to public relations."

"A good suit can take you places," agreed Gary, "not to mention an IS badge."

"In reply to your earlier question," Dr. Reickert said, "yes, it is possible to induce controlled earthquakes in regions along a fault line."

"How?" asked Morgana.

"To explain, I will have to give you a miniature lesson in geotechtonics." Gary listened attentively as Dr. Reickert explained. "Earthquakes are caused when two land plates rub against each other along a fault line. By injecting specified quantities of fluids—like water—at strategic points along the fault line, the plates can be artificially made to start moving. This is how we can induce earthquakes of specific strengths in specific regions."

"Water can cause earthquakes?" Morgana was incredulous.

Dr. Reickert ignored Morgana. "Now tell me where you want this earthquake induced, and why?"

"I will show you." Earthknight turned to Morgana. "You stay here until we get back."

"What do earthquakes have to do with fighting the aliens?" asked Morgana. "And I still don't believe you can cause earthquakes with water."

It took some time for Dr. Reickert to get used to flying over the land in the arms of Earthknight, but once she did, she started enjoying it.

"You know," she shouted over the whistling of the wind, "when I used to read those Superman comics and see Supes flying through the air with Lois Lane in his arms, I used to imagine myself in her place."

"So how are you today, Lois?" said Gary.

"Tops, Clarke."

They were nearing the spaceship.

"What I am going to show you, Dr. Reickert," said Gary, "is top secret."

"Susan," said Dr. Reickert.

"What?"

"Call me Susan."

Gary laughed.

"Why are you laughing?"

"What a time to get informal."

Far off in the horizon, just the tip of the alien spaceship could be seen.

"Anyway, as I was saying, Susan," Gary continued, "what I am going to show you is top secret. I hope they don't throw me into a federal prison for letting the cat out of the bag."

"What cat?"

Gary pointed below. "That cat."

There was shock and awe on Susan's face as she looked down and saw the spaceship and the dead bodies around it.

"What is that?" She whispered.

"It is an alien spaceship and they want to conquer earth, and…"

"And what?"

"And the spaceship is invulnerable to all of our weapons, as evidenced by the bodies of our dead soldiers around it."

Susan's face turned white. The sight of the battle torn bodies was not pleasant.

"Mark the spot, Susan," said Gary. "This is the answer to your questions about where and why. Now I want an answer to my question."

"The answer is, yes."

They turned back.

Susan led him to what seemed to be a bustling computer lab. People were busy on various instruments and terminals. Many faces turned curiously toward the man dressed in black armor. Quite a few of them seemed to recognize Earthknight and smiled and nodded as he passed

Ahmed A. Khan

by.

Susan grabbed an empty terminal and started tapping the keyboard. Gary watched from behind her chair as figures and shapes danced on the screen.

"Ah yes! Here we are," Susan declared happily. I have found the exact quantity of water that we need to inject and the exact spot where it should be done."

"Okay! Let's go," said Gary.

Earthknight and Susan once again stood outside the gate of the research station. Earthknight spread his arms wide to invite Susan to another flight.

"No," Susan declined with obvious regret. "This time, we'll have to travel by road."

"Why?"

"We'll have to take the water tanker."

"Oh!"

Earthknight and Susan moved to a water tanker on wheels.

Susan got into the truck and started it. Earthknight flew and Morgana followed in the air car.

They travelled for about a quarter of an hour.

Susan stopped the truck one point and climbed down. Earthknight and Morgana landed close to her. The far away silhouette of the spaceship could be seen from this spot.

"Here is a hole in the ground that leads to the fault," Susan pointed.

Gary dragged the hose from the tanker to the hole. Susan looked in the direction of the spaceship and started the pump. Morgana sat beside the hole, watching the water gushing into it. She turned and saw Gary still looking in the direction of the spaceship.

"Looking out for the fly swatter?" She grinned.

"That's enough water," Susan declared and stopped the pump. "Now let's make tracks."

Gary shut down the pump and started rolling the hose. Susan stopped him.

"Forget the tanker. There is not enough time to make our escape before it hits. Fly."

They flew, Susan in Earthknight's arms and Morgana in the air car.

They hovered over the spaceship as they watched and waited.

The ground below seemed to vibrate.

"Thar she blows!" Gary shouted.

The vibrations grew into tremors. The ground below the spaceship started to split open. Slowly, inexorably, the crack in the ground widened. It widened enough to cause the spaceship to tilt slightly. It widened enough to make the spaceship sink halfway through the ground. It widened enough to swallow the spaceship whole. And then it began to narrow down.

The aliens were strong but not strong enough to fight earth itself.

"A resounding success, don't you think?" Earthknight said as he removed his helmet. He was back in the air car with Morgana.

"Not at all a success," replied Morgana.

"What?"

"You did not follow the script," she said. "Your orders were to infiltrate, go aboard the ship somehow. And you failed. Now we don't even know what the aliens looked like and all their technology has been buried with them."

Suddenly, she burst into laughter. "And don't forget the fly swatter," she gasped.

Earthknight looked at her darkly.

"Some day, I will either kill you or marry you," he said.

Love and Life

Another original story, never before published, and another story produced because of a challenge I threw to myself. I will not go into details because the challenge is implicit in the story.

You sit staring at the blank screen of your laptop. To break or not to break the rules? Creativity or safety? It is a heady and scary thought.

Numerous stories are born daily, and almost all stories contain in them at least one interesting twist of the plot. How about a story with no twist at all? How about a story which describes a straight line on the page of life? Is such a story possible?

A deep, dark precipice looms. You jump over the precipice and start to type.

There was/is/will be a girl called Bel.

Bel was an ordinary girl. That is to say, there were millions of girls in the world like her, and there was no girl in the world like her.

She had a nice face and figure and a lively personality, but her face could not launch a small sail-boat, let alone a thousand ships. Her eyes had not the depth of a small pond, let alone the oceans, but those eyes could see and be seen. Her eyes could not make lightning strike the heart of one who looked at them, but they could arouse soft, delicate feelings in it. Her hair was black and long, but it looked neither like a snake when plaited, nor like a cloud when loose.

Her face usually looked fresh, but sometimes it became dull. She had a good dress sense, but sometimes the dresses she wore made her look idiotic.

Bel loved to read. She liked children. She liked gardening.

In short, she was a reasonably attractive, reasonably intelligent and reasonably sensible girl.

The speakers on your console squawk: CODE YELLOW. YOU ARE IN VIOLATION OF AN IMPORTANT RULE: SHOW, DO NOT TELL. IF YOU PERSIST, YOU WILL BE PUNISHABLE BY LAW.

You continue typing.

If there was/is/will be a girl called Bel then there was/is/will be a boy called Bo.

Bo was an ordinary boy. That is to say, there were millions of boys in the world like him, and there was no boy in the world like him.

Bo was good looking, but an Apollo he was not. He was intelligent enough to be in the top ten students in his college if he tried hard enough, but he was not intelligent enough to locate errors in Einstein's theories at the drop of a hat. In fact, he was not intelligent enough even to keep his tongue under his control all the time. He was crazy about books, but not so much that he could not enjoy a game of football or Chinese checkers.

He was strong enough to break someone's jaw in a fight, but he was not strong enough to fight two or three persons at a time and come out of it without a crease on his clothes.

There was a slight childishness in him which sometimes looked attractive and other times looked silly.

I do not know how Bo and Bel met each other. It is possible that they knew each other from their childhood. They may even have been related to each other. Or it is equally possible that they came to know each other in their college days. I do not know anything about it. All I know is that when they saw each other for the first time, there was no thunder or lightning in their hearts. No fireworks went off in their head. Time did not stop for them. They did not feel as if that was the moment they had been waiting for all their lives.

The speakers go: YOU ARE COMPOUNDING YOUR FELONY BY PERSISTING IN TELLING, NOT SHOWING. DESIST IMMEDI- ATELY.

All that happened after they met was that they continued meeting. A feeling of mutual admiration and respect developed between them.

They came close to each other but there were no clandestine meetings between them. There was no fervent declaration of undying love.

They did not tell each other that one of them just could not bear to live without the other. They knew that they were each other's friends, not each other's food, water and air.

He never said to her that if he could not marry her, he would never marry anyone else. Neither did she say anything of the sort to him. Both of them were quite sensible individuals and knew that they could not have full control over their future. Then suppose, due to some reason, they could not marry each other? What would happen? Would they truly remain bachelors all their lives? It would be an unnatural and stupid thing to do. Then would they marry elsewhere? Would not that mean that they would break their promise? What was the use of such a promise? Bo and Bel were not the heroes and heroines of cheap novel, and so they were able to think through all these ramifications of life and to express their ideas to each other.

The speakers squawk again: CODE RED. THERE CANNOT BE A STORY WITHOUT A CONFLICT. YOU ARE GOING AGAINST THE PRIME DIRECTIVE. REVISE IMMEDIATELY TO AVOID PENALIZATION.

It is too late to stop. You type faster.

And so, denying all opportunities of a twist in the plot, our story moves forward in a straight line, coming close to its momentary conclusion.

Bo and Bel got married.

I have heard that Bo is happy with his wife. They love each other, and are leading a peaceful life.

I have also heard that Bel is happy with her husband. They love each other and are leading quite a peaceful life.

What I have not heard and what I do not know is whether Bo's wife is Bel or some other girl and whether Bel's husband is Bo or some other boy.

However, Bo is Bo and Bel is Bel and both of them are/were/will be lovable kids.

You end the story and with a mixed sense of triumph and dread, press the button that will cast your story out on the cyber waves, accessible for everyone.

The speakers are saying: EDITORS ARE ON THEIR WAY. RESISTING ARREST IS FUTILE.

You hear the sounds of sirens coming closer and closer.

Ahmed A. Khan

Point Counter Point

In an introduction to one of his books, Neil Gaiman wrote that he was writing a story in collaboration with Harlan Ellison. He went on to say that each time they worked together on the story, the story seemed to grow smaller. And this comment of Gaiman's became the spark that touched off the chain reaction of creativity. How far could a story be reduced?

This is another one of my stories appearing here for the first time.

I started to write a story. It turned out to be an allegory. It started like this:

In my journey I came across a huge expanse of desert. In the middle of the desert, I found Atlas standing bent under the weight of the heavens that he carried on his broad shoulders. He looked tired and miserable.
"Will you relieve me?" he asked.
I was strong enough.
"Okay," I said.

I then took a break and went about the business of life.
"There should be child in the story," my spouse said later.
So I deleted one line from the story and added another one.

"Will you relieve me?" he asked.
"Okay," I said. My child would help me with my burden if needed.

Time went by.
I deleted the last two sentences of the story and replaced them with one sentence.

"Will you relieve me?" he asked.
"No," I said, and kicked him in his shins.

More time went by.
"We must have the child back in the story and the child should grow up."
I went back to the second version of the story and added to it.

"Will you relieve me?" he asked.

"Okay," I said. My child would help me with my burden.

A few years went by. I was getting tired of the heavens on my shoulders. I looked at my child, now grown up and strong, playing in the sand.

"Help me," I called to him.

He looked at me once, then turned back and continued playing.

When next I had time, I revised the story and ended up with what turned out to be its longest, almost complete, version.

The story now went like this:

In my journey I came across a huge expanse of desert. In the middle of the desert, I found Atlas standing bent under the weight of the heavens that he carried on his broad shoulders. He looked at the world I carried on my shoulders. It looked small.

"Exchange?" he asked.

"Okay," I said.

So we exchanged our weights and Atlas merrily walked away as I stood alone in the middle of the desert, holding the heavens aloft.

Time passed.

Then I saw Atlas staggering towards me.

"Take back your world," he panted.

The bearer of the heavens was staggering under the weight of my world.

I smiled. We exchanged our burdens and I resumed my journey.

With time I learned.

I looked at the story. It was too long. So I went back to the first version of my story and started cutting away anything that sounded even remotely superfluous and ended up with this:

In my journey, I came across Atlas standing bent under the weight of the heavens. He looked at the world on my shoulders.

"Exchange?" he asked.

"Okay," I said.

I pondered. The story could be shortened further.

I gave relief to Atlas.

"Why not give it a more general, more universal object?"

I gave relief.

"Make it still more general."

I gave.

"More."

I.

I looked at my story and realized that even that single mono-alpha-betical, monosyllabic word was nothing more nor less than a symbol — a symbol for the eternal, the infinite, the indefinable reality.

So I removed the symbol.

.

Synchronicity

This story is so different from all the other stories I have written that I had a very hard time selling it until Vulgata finally bought it and published it and paid me good money. One of the highlights of my writing career happened when a reader commented that this was one of the most life affirming stories he had ever read in his life (and the reader was over 60).

Dawn

Anil Kapadia, thirty-three, part time writer and full time computer consultant, sat eating his breakfast, then picked up his glass of water and poured it over his head. Shocked at his own action, he started laughing.

This was the start of an interesting chain of causes and effects.

The day had started with Anil opening his eyes to a beautiful Saturday morning in the midst of August. His mind still clouded with sleep, he tried to snuggle up to his wife and remembered that his wife had gone to stay with her parents after a fight with him last week. They had fought over something silly, so silly that he had already forgotten what the bone of contention was. Anil had a sneaking suspicion that in that fight, he had been the one who was more in the wrong. So the first emotion that he felt that morning was a twinge of guilt. But then the world intruded upon his senses.

The window drapes had lighted up. He went to the window and pulled them back. The light fell on his young but slightly haggard face. He opened the window. A cool breeze played around his face while he, with his fingers, tried unsuccessfully to brush his unruly hair into some semblance of order.

An ancient book had described dawn thus: By the first ray of rising sun, the world is stirred. Shining gold is sprinkled on smiling flowers. The fragrant air is filled with sweet melodies of singing birds.

Well, this morning was not wholly as described in the ancient book. The fragrance of the air was a teeny bit diluted by the smell of garbage and car fumes. The sounds of moving cars and shouting juvenile delinquents sometimes overwhelmed the sweet melodies of singing birds. Yet it was a good enough morning all in all, except for the fact that his loneliness of the moment depressed him.

His apartment was on the third floor of a high-rise building. His window overlooked a tree-lined street that was moderately busy in the day but almost totally deserted during the night. On his side of the street was a row of apartment buildings. On the other side of the street was a huge shopping plaza.

He stood at the window for some time, watching the traffic on the street below. Then he turned and walked to the bathroom. It was while he was in the shower and warm water sprayed over every pore of his body that a strange kind of self-awareness hit him. He felt as if his soul had split in two: an observer and the observed. He watched himself taking the shower and thought: "What am I doing here?"

The "here" in his thought did not stand for the shower, nor did it stand for his apartment. It had nothing to do with his present time and place as in "here and now." The "here" in this particular thought stood for the world, the universe, his whole existence.

Strangeness followed strangeness. He had a premonition, an expectation. Something significant was going to happen to him that day. But what? He had no clue whatsoever.

The feeling of expectation was still there while he busied himself with breakfast. He picked up two slices of bread. Popped them in the toaster. Opened the fridge and took out the packet of butter. The slices popped out of toaster, burned black. He threw the slices in the trash can. Picked up two more slices. Popped them in the toaster. Adjusted the toaster to the correct temperature. The slices popped out, well done this time. He put them on a plate. Applied butter. Carried the plate to the table. Flopped down on the chair. At last the ordeal was over and his breakfast was ready.

He thought wistfully of his wife.

At about the same time, a few miles away from Anil's place, at the house of his in-laws, his wife Jasmine was thinking about him wistfully. I wonder how he is managing without me, she mused. The housework must have reduced the poor guy to jitters. It has now been nearly a week and he has not come to woo me back. The fight had been his mistake. He should apologize to me and make it up to me and may be, just may be, I will forgive him this time. But then, what was it that Erich Segal had written in "Love Story?" "Love means not having to say sorry", or something like that, wasn't it?

And furthermore, how could he come here? Her parents had moved to this new house just last week and Anil did not know the address. But then he did know the telephone number here. He could have at least called, the jerk.

Flames

Anil remembered that last night, before going to sleep, he had mentally made a list of things that he had to do the next day. But somehow, in the light of the day, he seemed to have forgotten everything that had been on his mind the night before. All he remembered was a dream. He had dreamt that he had gone to the house of his in-laws with the intention of making up with his wife. He had reached the house, parked his car in front of the house, gone up the driveway and pushed the bell. His wife had opened the door. "What took you so long?" she had said and moved into his arms. And it had felt so good. And then he had woken up.

He picked up a pen and a paper and tried to jot down the things he had to do that day. Nothing in the way of pending actions came to his mind. Instead, what did come to mind was a philosophical statement from Bhagvad Gita.

"Only actions done in God bind not the soul of man."

And he felt the weight of the fetters on his soul and the weight oppressed him.

He remembered the flame sermon of Buddha.

"Everything, O people, is aflame. And how, O people, is everything aflame? I declare unto you that it is aflame with the fire of lust, with the fire of anger, with the fire of ignorance. It is aflame with the anxieties of birth, decay, death, grief, suffering, dejection and despair.

"The eye is aflame, visible objects are aflame.

"The ear is aflame, sounds are aflame.

"The nose is aflame, odors are aflame.

"The tongue is aflame, tastes are aflame.

"The body is aflame, objects of contact are aflame.

"The mind is aflame, thoughts are aflame."

How do you quench the flames? He thought. With water, of course. It all seemed so logical at that time. He simply picked up a glass of water from the dining table and poured it over his head.

While his mind had been waxing philosophical, there had been a knock on the door, but he had been too absorbed in his thoughts to hear it. It was his next door neighbor, Tony Wilson. Tony and Anil were close to each other, so when he knocked and Anil did not open his door, he tried the handle and finding it unlocked, simply opened the door and walked in, right at the moment when Anil, his back to the door, was pouring water over his head. He watched this sight with eyes agog, then tiptoed out, slowly closing the door behind him.

An extremely worried Tony returned to his apartment. Something was seriously wrong with Anil. The estrangement from his wife seemed to have unhinged him slightly. What should he do? What was his duty as Anil's friend? He thought of their mutual friend, Dr. Ali. Yes, he was the right person to call for help. Tony picked up the telephone and dialled Ali's number.

Premonition

Anil laughed at himself for his silly action, got up and changed his clothes and sat down at his computer. First, he surfed the Net for the latest news. There was a lot of it: murder, war, politics, promiscuity.

Anil, who was feeling depressed already, felt even more depressed. He quickly got off the news page and opened up his email account. Immediately, he was hit with the dilemma he had been facing the previous day.

At his place of work, by sheer accident he had uncovered the fact that his boss was dealing in drugs. His nature screamed at him to have this fact exposed to the world. He had a journalist friend and one email to this friend would be enough to open this can of worms. But he was afraid — afraid of losing his job, afraid even of his life. What if his boss had gangster connections and had him killed or beaten or maimed? And he hated himself for being afraid.

He shut off his browser and opened up the word processor, wanting to work on his novel. This book he was writing was overtly idealistic. It spoke of morals, ethics, values. It even talked of God.

No one is going to publish it, he thought. Why am I writing?

He was about to shut off the computer in disgust when Bhagvad Gita once again came to his aid.

"You have the right to works, not to their fruits. They are surely to be pitied who hanker after the fruit of every action. May failure or success be one to you. Even an iota of righteousness in your actions shall deliver you from cosmic fear. Plunge into action and leave the result to God. The wise who merge their intellect in Him are freed forever from the bondage of birth."

He picked up his writing where he had left it. He was still in the early chapters of his book. At that particular moment, he was at the point of describing the interior of the apartment of his hero. Now, how do I want the guy's apartment to look? Take from life. Why do I not put down the description of my own apartment?

He cast a look around and started to write.

It was a two-bedroom apartment. The walls were white. The floor was covered with a blue carpet.

In the master bedroom, the double bed lay snug against the wall opposite the window, covered with sky blue curtains and golden drapes. The window opened to the east and in the morning, sometimes when he got up before his wife, he would draw the curtains aside, and sunlight would fall directly on the bed, lighting up the rumpled comfortably slept-in sheets, and the painfully beautiful sight of his sleeping wife, her dark hair spread on her pillow in soft curls. The second bedroom awaited the coming of his progeny to be put to its proper use. Currently, the spare bedroom was used as a study and shelves full of books lined most of its walls.

Anil stopped typing. The premonition, the expectancy of something significant in the air, returned with renewed vigor.

Be aware, he commanded himself. Aware of self and surroundings. Aware of the texture of your clothes on your body. Aware of the patterns that the sunlight seeping through the windows created on the furniture and fixtures of the room. Aware of the indescribable taste of cool clear water as it passed through the lips, over the tongue and into the throat. Aware of the smells all around. Aware of the dim sounds from the street below.

Be aware. Aware of what you are. Aware of your position in the universe. Aware of the motivators of your actions. Aware of what was right and what was not.

The telephone rang. Anil picked it up. It was his mother and she sounded worried.

"Hi, Mom."

"Your father," she sobbed.

Ahmed A. Khan

"What happened?" he almost shouted.

"He is being operated today."

"Operated? What for?"

"Appendicitis."

"What time is the operation?"

"At two."

"I will be there, Mom. Don't worry. Everything will be all right."

He put down the phone and sat there for quite a while, not moving, his heart palpitating with worry.

"Mom. Dad." He spoke softly, imagining they were right there in front him, not old as they were at present, but young and lively as they had been when he was a child.

I wish Mom and Dad had agreed to come and live with me, he thought. He had asked them, pleaded with them many times, but every time they had refused. Every time the answer was the same.

"This is the place we grew up. All our memories are here. There is a part of us in each nook and cranny of this house, each alley, each street here."

"Then I will come and live with you and find a job somewhere near you." He had said.

"No. No need to sacrifice your excellent job for us. You worry needlessly. We will be fine here. And of course you will be visiting us every now and then during the weekends."

He did not remember who had said those words. Was it his father or his mother? It did not matter. They spoke with one tongue. Will our love for each other—my wife's and mine—be as strong in our old age?

My wife. I will call her right now. This illness of my father is the right pretext. Our quarrel will be forgotten. She will come to me. She loves my parents.

He was about to pick up the receiver and dial the number of his in-laws when the door opened and Dr. Ali walked in.

Detour

Dr. Ali was a strange character. Highly intelligent, sharp witted, incisive, an expert neurologist. And he was an idealist of the first order. It was this idealism that had made Anil see a kindred soul in Dr.

Ali. They had hit if off extremely well right from their first meeting which had taken place when Anil had gone to consult him about a minor neurological problem that he was having.

Ali was one of those doctors, quite rare these days, who take their Hippocratic oath quite seriously. He was from a poor family. His parents suffered great hardships to give their son an opportunity to succeed in the world..

Anil was surprised to see Ali.

"Hey, Doc." He smiled with genuine pleasure.

There was no answering smile from Ali. Instead, he looked at Anil steadily.

"What are you staring at me for?"

"Are you feeling well, Anil?" There was extreme concern and worry in Ali's voice.

"Feeling well? Of course I am feeling well. At least I was until you walked in."

"Sure?"

"What is this?" Anil was alarmed.

Ali ignored his question.

"Won't you ask me to sit and offer me something to eat?"

"Do I have to ask you? My house is yours, dear friend, as the spider said to the fly." Anil laughed. "But then, you can hardly find something decent to eat in this house right now, with Jasmine away."

Ali sat down on the sofa. "Speaking of Jasmine, haven't you patched up your quarrel with her by now?"

"N-no, not yet, but…Oh! By the way, you will have to excuse me for a moment. I have to make a phone call to my travel agent."

"Travel agent? What for?"

"I am taking the noon flight to visit my parents."

"All of a sudden?"

"Yeah! I Just got a call from Mom. Dad's going to have his appendix removed."

"Oh!"

Anil went to make his phone call. Ali sat there, thinking hard. First, the problem with his wife. And now this. His father's surgery. A second big blow. Enough to unhinge a sensitive person.

Ali got up abruptly and disconnected the phone. Anil looked at him with surprise.

"Why'd you do that? I had not completed my travel arrangements."

"I cannot allow you to travel at this moment."

"What?"

"I think you are about to have a nervous breakdown, and I want to take you to my hospital for a check up."

"A nervous breakdown? Nonsense. What gave you that idea?"

"Tell you later, but you have to come with me."

"But I cannot. I have to take the noon flight. Dad's operation is at two. I want to be there before the operation."

"Look. There is another flight out at about two. I will finish your check up in time for you to catch that flight. You will be there while the operation is going on. That is the best I can do."

"Damn you, okay I will come with you to your blasted hospital," Anil shouted, raw anger in his voice.

Martyrdom

The day was bright. Overhead, the sky was clear. Traffic moved on the road at an even pace. Anil sat in Ali's car, brooding, oblivious to the pleasant weather outside even as he subconsciously registered the first indications of the oncoming fall. Parts of the tree-lined sidewalks were covered by a crinkly carpet of gold and red leaves.

As their car turned from the main road into a side street, they saw a procession going by. The people were all wearing black and they were carrying banners. Two words were prominent on the banners: "Hussain" and "Karbala".

Anil stopped brooding and looked at the procession with interest.

"These are your people, aren't they? Muslims?"

"Yes," Ali nodded.

"What kind of procession is this?"

"It is a procession to mourn and commemorate the martyrdom of Hussain ibn Ali."

"And who is—or was—Hussain ibn Ali?"

"He was the grandson of Mohammed, the Messenger of Allah. He was martyred fighting for the right against overwhelming odds in a place called Karbala in Iraq, fourteen centuries ago on the tenth of the Islamic month of Muharram. Today is that date. The Muslims commemorate this day every year to keep alive the ideals of Hussain that teach never to bow down before tyranny."

"Tell me more about Hussain." The writer in Anil was intrigued.

"A tyrant by the name of Yazid ibn Muawiya had declared himself ruler of Muslims. He demanded allegiance from Hussain because allegiance from the grandson of the Prophet would legitimize all Yazid's oppressions and debauchery. Hussain refused. A fight ensued."

"Oh, so it was a fight for power."

"No. Hussain made sure that no unbiased historian could ever label the battle of Karbala as a fight for power or kingdom. He did not take any army with them. Instead, he took a group of about a hundred people, including his family and close companions. To them he declared that he was going to his death. It is better to die an honourable death, he said, than live under oppression. He said it was his fight and urged them not to accompany him, but they refused to leave him."

"So what happened?"

"Well, in Karbala, besides the banks of the river Euphrates, Hussain and his companions faced Yazid's army. The least head count given in books for Yazid's army in Karbala is thirty thousand. These thirty thousand soldiers blocked Hussain and his family and friends, including small children, from the waters of Euphrates. For three days, people in Hussain's camp went thirsty. This was a tactic to pressure Hussain in accepting Yazid's rule. Well, the tactic failed. A fight ensued. Hussain and his followers were martyred and members of his family, including women and children were made prisoners. But since then, this sacrifice has become a beacon of inspiration for free thinkers all over the world.

"A poet, in a couplet, said it well: Hussain, you lost your life and your family, but you made it possible for us never to fear an oppressor."

There was silence in the car until they reached the hospital.

Hospital

Their car stopped at the hospital. Anil followed Ali into the hospital. In the lobby, two old ladies, obviously patients, seemed to be having a reunion. They saw each other. Their eyes lit up. They moved towards each other, arms outstretched. They embraced, the wrinkles on their faces surrounding their smiles like illuminations found on the margins of old and antique books. Even in his troubled state, the writer in Anil could not help noticing this scene and filing it for future use in his novel.

Anil was put through a number of tests. There were neurological tests, physical tests, neurophysical tests and more. His reflexes were tested. His IQ was tested.

Noon came and went.

In between the tests, Anil shouted for Ali.

"What is it?" Ali asked.

"I want to call Mom."

On the phone, he said: "Mom, I am afraid I cannot catch today's flight."

"It's okay, Baba" she replied. "In fact, there is no need for you to come. It is a minor operation. Nothing to worry about," she consoled Anil, but her voice betrayed her worry.

"I'll be there first thing tomorrow, Mom," he said and put down the phone.

After a battery of tests, it was time for lunch. During lunch, he asked Ali, "Now tell me what is this all about? Why all these tests?"

"We felt that you had been under great tension the past few days."

"We?"

"Tony and I."

"Oh Tony! Where does he come into the story?"

"He saw you doing something nonsensical."

"Like what?"

"Like pouring a glass of water over your head."

"Oh my God!"

After lunch there were a few more tests. After the completion of other tests, he was even subjected to a session of psychoanalysis. Somehow, he found the session with the psychoanalyst quite rewarding. The psychoanalyst asked several questions. Questions like:

How was your childhood?

Tell us about your friends.

Do you love your wife?

What is your goal in life? What do you want to get out of life?

He gave one line responses to these questions, but the backdrop that his mind supplied to each of his responses was detailed and complex:.

Childhood

My childhood? What do I remember about my childhood? Quite a lot, in fact. Probably, the reason is that the child I was is still a part of me.

A sprawling, yellow old-fashioned house with tiled roofs was where I lived. The house sported a garden. There were numerous fruits and flowers in the garden. In the midst of the garden there was a small water pond around which lilies grew.

Paddy fields—no, they did not belong to us—stretched for several acres in front of our house. To reach the fields, all you had to do was cross the road. This road led to the railway station which was about two minutes walk from our house. Sitting in the house, we could hear the sounds of the coming and going trains. The railway tracks passed through the paddy fields. I enjoyed seeing the trains passing through the green fields.

A part of my day was spent in school. The rest was spent in various things: doing my homework, playing, climbing trees, reading comic books and fairy tales, finding an isolated spot in the house and sitting there quietly, imagining myself to be—as my mood directed me—Tarzan, Robinson Crusoe, or Robur the Conqueror.

In the evening, all of us, father, mother, grandfather, grandmother (ours was an extended family) would either take a walk or bring out chairs and sit in front of the house in the gathering coolness of the night, gossiping. It was pleasant.

Summer nights in our house were extra special. Some of us—particularly my grandmother and myself—would sleep in the open, on wooden cots covered with crisp, clean sheets. It was extremely pleasant lying there in the coolness of the night, staring up at the star-studded sky and listening to the snores of the rest of the sleepers and the chirruping of crickets, grasshoppers and other insects, while the fragrance of spring flowers filled my nostrils.

During holidays, my afternoons were usually spent in grandfather's room. I would lie beside him on his bed and he would tell me stories of great thinkers of the world—and I would lie there assimilating it all, occasionally asking him a question, otherwise remaining silent.

After the story session, he would usually go to sleep and I would get up from his bed and go prowling around in his room, searching for any books of his that I had not read. I would invariably find one book or the other and start reading it at once, sitting in his armchair. These books were usually quite old ones, their bindings torn, their pages termite eaten, and a strange sort of smell rising up from them—a mysterious, magical smell.

Have you ever noticed what books, particularly old books, smell of? They smell of sunny and cloudy days and dark and moonlit nights. They smell of battle-fields and gardens, of open skies and dusty attics, of deserts and mountains, of destinies and purpose. They smell of time.

Friends

I remember a time late one night, Ali and I sat on a bench in the park near my house.

We started talking about artificiality in our lives.

"Self deception is our darling," I said. We do not have the guts to criticise ourselves. There is artificiality in our thinking, in our actions. How can we be free of this artificiality?"

At last, Ali spoke: "If one can come out of the circle of self then one is free."

I thought over this statement. "Yes. But self is insidious. It gets into everything and pollutes purity."

"How?"

"Take worship. What kind of worship of God do you think is more laudatory: worship that is done to get rewards from God, worship that is done in fear of punishment, or worship that is done out of love of God?"

"I get your drift. It brings to mind a saying of Ali ibn Abi Talib."

"Who is Ali ibn Abi Talib?"

"He was the successor of our Prophet Muhammad."

"And what is the saying?"

"Well, Ali had said that if one worships God in hope of heaven, this is the worship of businessmen; if one worships God in fear of hell, this is the worship of slaves; and if one worships God because He is worth worshipping, this is the worship of a free person."

"There you are. That is the freedom I am talking about—freedom from the circle of self."

Jasmine

She is the daughter of a friend of my father.

The first time I met her was when I had completed my undergraduate degree and was lazing around the house, feeling pretty bored while I waited for the summer holidays to end and my Masters program to begin. My father suggested I spend some days at the farmhouse of his friend. I accepted his suggestion.

My first day at the farmhouse, I met a lively young lady who was introduced to me as Jasmine, the daughter of the house. She had been studying abroad and had just completed her under grad degree as well.

My second day at the farmhouse, I woke up in the morning, went to the bathroom and gave a blood curdling scream because someone had painted a huge moustache on my face.

My third day there, I found missing from my things a book (a Thorne Smith novel) and an unfinished short story of mine. The next day, I found both the items. Along with the book was a note that said, "You seem to have good taste in your reading." But the most surprising thing was my unfinished story. It was unfinished no longer. It had been completed, and completed in a brilliant way.

I knew who was behind all this mischief. Jasmine, of course. What could I do but marry her?

Significant Event?

The psychoanalysis session over, Anil turned to Ali.

"Can I leave now," his tone was sarcastic, "or are you taking me to a mental institution?"

Ali smiled. "You have to admit Tony was right in worrying about you. That's what friends are for."

"With friends like you two..." Anil left the expression incomplete, but he smiled.

"I'll drop you home. Just wait here for a while. I have to get rid of some paperwork at my office." Ali left. Anil waited in the lobby. He did not have long to wait. Within minutes, he saw Ali rushing towards him.

Ahmed A. Khan

"Did you hear the news?"

"What news?" Anil asked.

"The flight that you were supposed to take today, it crashed and everyone on board died."

"Oh my God!"

Ali just gave him a look. In that look was shock—shock at the thought of what might have happened to Anil if he had taken that flight. In that look was wonder—wonder at the chain of unlikely events that had saved Anil's life.

Was this the significant event in my life that I had premonition of? Anil wondered, but then, the feeling of something about to happen still persisted in him.

They reached Anil's house. Anil called Tony over. At first, Tony appeared sheepish over his role in the day's events, but when Ali told him of the net result of the events, he became jubilant.

"Be eternally grateful to me, my boy," he said grandiosely. "I saved your life today."

"And just for that you deserve death punishment, Tony," said Ali.

"I see your point," said Tony thoughtfully. Anil punched him in the arm, went into the kitchen and came out with lemonade and glasses. They sipped the lemonade, talked, and then Ali and Tony left, leaving Anil alone with his thoughts.

Dusk

Anil called his mother and breathed a sigh of relief to find that the operation had gone well and his father was doing fine.

He then booted up his computer and got online. "You made it possible for us never to fear an oppressor." Ali's words echoed in his ears. He sent off an email to his journalist friend—told him about his boss and his drug trafficking, felt a weight being lifted from his soul.

Dusk fell. Inevitably, Anil's thoughts turned to Jasmine. And suddenly, he had had enough of his stubbornness. He picked up the phone and dialed the number of his in-laws. There was no response from the other side. Some problem with the line perhaps. He put down the receiver and stood there silently, wringing his hands. Then he made a decision.

I am going out there to get Jasmine back, he said to himself and came out of the house. It was dusk and the world was lit with the mixed light of the setting sun and the street lamps.

It was only when his car had left the driveway of the building and had moved onto the road that he realized he did not know where Jasmine's parents lived.

In anguish, he decided to turn back when he suddenly remembered his dream in which he had driven up to the new house of his in-laws and met Jasmine. He remembered it all vividly and on a wild impulse, he let his car retrace the dream path. From one road to another, from one landmark to another, his car moved, the way it had moved in his dream. A long time passed. Suddenly, he saw a house in front of him —the same house that he had seen in the dream. He stopped the car, jumped out and walked towards the house, his whole being filled with a sense of wonder. He walked past the main gate. He walked past the beautiful garden. He walked past the portico. He climbed up the steps to the door. He rang the bell.

And Jasmine opened the door.

"What took you so long?" she asked.

Anil spread his arms and Jasmine stepped forward and into the outstretched arms.

"Let's go home?" Anil asked. Jasmine nodded.

Night

"There are few things like a good, clean fuck to put life in its proper perspective," someone had once written, and that night, Anil attested to the truth of this observation.

Pretty soon, Anil and Jasmine lay sweaty and sated in each other's arms. Jasmine slept, a soft smile playing on her lips.

Anil wallowed for sometime in euphoria as a welcome relaxation spread through his limbs and made them pleasantly heavy. Just before he went to sleep, he thought over the events of the day and realized that there had been not one, but many events of significance spread all over the day, including that event of a while ago—the act of copulation.

Anil did not know it then, but that night another significant event had taken place. First steps had been taken towards the creation of a new life in Jasmine's womb.

Ahmed A. Khan

T. Gips and the Time Flies

This story is light stuff—light and fun. All modesty aside, I think the "time flies" are a pretty nifty piece of imagination. This story appears here for the first time.

No one knows his real name.

At one time he had been called The Great Problem Solver or TGPS for short. Then the TGPS got transformed into T. Gips, and this name had stuck.

Whenever and wherever the known universe has an unsolvable problem, the first (or sometimes the last) person people think of is T. Gips. He charges a lot, but more often than not, he delivers.

T. Gips had just solved a problem of grave proportions on the planet Sisimak and was on his way to his home world of Elbracket when he received an SOS from Space Colony #203, the planet known as Enbond. He sighed and changed his flight plans. He was now on his way to Enbond to help the colonists there with some trouble caused by native insectoids called—such a strange name—time flies.

Dreading the moment, he called his wife, Jojo, on the Intergalactic Communicator. Jojo's youthful, smiling face appeared on the screen. She looked so ravishing, T. Gips fell in love all over again.

"When are you coming back home?" she came straight to the point.

"I—I was on my way home," he stopped, took a deep breath and continued. "But I have received an SOS from Enbond."

Jojo's smile vanished. "Mr. Gips, you are dead," she said icily and disconnected.

T. Gips sighed. Getting back into Jojo's good books would be a problem, probably greater than the one he had just solved on Sisimak or the one he would attempt to solve on Enbond.

His thoughts moved back to Enbond. He hoped he would not be bored there. He hoped he would at least be able to practice his archery—one of his many hobbies.

His ship emerged from hyperspace. Enbond was close at hand.

An hour later, T. Gips was sitting in the main dome, in the office of Administrator Robb Javins, discussing the problem of the time flies with him. "We had some time flies in our bio lab in this dome," said Dr. Javins, a portly man with a face that would have been called merry at normal times. Right now, all it showed was stress. "They were kept in a stasis chamber. They got out. Sheer negligence of a lab assistant, you know."

The dome was constructed on a hillside at quite a high altitude. The clear windows of the office overlooked a huge forest way down the hillside. Enbond was a forest world, full of interesting life forms.

"Why are these insects called time flies?" T. Gips asked.

"Because anything they touch is transported through time," said Javins, watching T. Gips' face for his reaction. He was not disappointed. A startled "What?" escaped T. Gips' lips.

They were interrupted by sounds. Buzz-crackle-pop, buzz-crackle-pop, the sounds went, starting low but slowly increasing in volume. Even as they watched, the wall on one side of the office developed fly-sized holes through which flies zoomed in. Some of them landed on the table, and as T. Gips watched, parts of the table started vanishing. Very soon the table surface was pock-marked.

Meanwhile, Javins had jumped out of his seat and was heading with great speed for the door. His speed was truly admirable in view of his girth.

"Run," he shouted, even as he put his words into practice. T. Gips ran.

"So where does the time-transported matter go?" T. Gips asked while he ran beside Javins. "Forward or backward in time?"

"Forward. That is how they feed."

"Explain."

"There is a release of energy related with transporting matter forward in time. The flies absorb this energy."

"Indigenous?"

"Yes, and thank God, they remain at lower levels and never move to higher altitudes, else our dome would not have survived."

"Interesting. Okay, what do you expect me to do?"

"Catch the escaped flies."

"Can't you kill them?"

"How? They are virtually untouchable. Anything touching them gets transported in time." They had to stop running because they had reached the end of the corridor.

"And," T. Gips prompted.

"And we are hoping you can find a way to get them back into the stasis chamber."

"How?"

"Aren't you the great problem solver? So solve."

T. Gips thought hard, and thought fast. The time flies were following them. He could once again hear the buzz-crackle-popping sounds.

He snapped his fingers. He had the answer.

"Come with me," he said, and raced toward the room that had been assigned to him as his living quarters.

Inside the room, he opened his bag and pulled out his archery set. He grabbed an arrow and handed it to Javins.

"Quick, put this arrow in the stasis chamber."

"What?" Javins exploded.

"Quick, man. Don't waste time!"

Uncomprehending, but with a what-the-hell air, Javins hurried toward the bio lab, closely followed by T. Gips. They entered the lab. Sounds indicated that the time flies were close behind them. Very close behind them. Almost upon them, actually. Javins turned to look. The flies had entered the lab and seemed to be making straight for them.

Still not knowing how it could save them, Javins threw the arrow into the stasis chamber. Immediately, the flies changed direction and homed in on the arrow. Within moments, they were all safely inside the chamber and Javins quickly sealed it.

"What was that all about?" Javins, still incredulous, asked T. Gips once they were back in Javin's office and had gotten their breaths back. "What made you so sure that an arrow would lure them into the stasis chamber?"

"Haven't you heard," explained T. Gips, "that time flies like an arrow?"

T. Gips left. He had solved another problem, but his mind was already on the next one. What could he say or do to get back into Jojo's good books?

The Book of Pain

If anyone asked me to select my top five stories, this story is sure to be included. (Incidentally, the other 4 of my stories that I consider my best are all included in this collection. Down the road, I will point out one of these 4 and I will let the readers form their guesses about the other three.) This story was first published in Anotherealm in 2000. It was reprinted in the "Dana Literary Journal" and reprinted again in "Ragged Edge" (another defunct market) where it won the "Best of the Best" award.

The gods silently assessed the new candidate and nodded to each other. He looked promising. Then one of them spoke.

"Time for the test. Are you ready?"

"Yes," said the new-comer.

"It will be painful," warned the god. The other gods chuckled. "Good pun, good pun," they applauded.

"Pun?" the new-comer was confused.

"Come with me," said the god who had spoken to him. He led the new-comer to the mouth of a huge pit.

"Look within," the god said.

The new-comer looked. In the pit, he saw a huge, seething and swarming pile of..something indescribable. This pile was immense, almost reaching the boundaries of infinity, and it was still growing. The sight of it made him feel uneasy.

"What is it?" he asked.

"It is Pain," said the god.

"Pain?"

"Pain. Created as a result of certain unwise actions of creatures throughout the universe. Ever-growing through a chain of cause and effect. What you see before you is a reservoir of all the Pain in the universe. You are given the job of handling this Pain for two celestial days. In this time, dispense with the Pain completely and as you see fit. This is your test," and then the god gave him a book.

"This book will be your guide. Read it and act wisely." Saying this, the god walked away, leaving the new-comer to his own thoughts.

The new-comer started taking stock of the situation. What was the quantity of Pain present? What was its rate of growth? Among how many creatures was it to be distributed? Who was to get what kind of Pain and how much of it?

He looked at the book the god had given to him. Its title was "The

Book of Pain."

He opened the book.

The first page of the book gave him all the statistical data he needed about the pile of Pain. From the second page onwards, the main body of the book started. It was divided into several untitled chapters. The book went thus:

Chapter 1

Pain punishes.

No unrepented evil deed goes unpunished, for as you sow, so shall you reap.

And the Punisher can be as subtle as he wishes.

(Further reading: "The Water Babies", by Charles Kingsley, especially the parts of the book featuring the two fairies called Do-as-you-be-done-by and Be-done-by-as-you-did.)

Chapter 2

Pain teaches.

Come near and listen to a story.

Once upon a time, there was a nice and tender-hearted boy. This tender-hearted boy was extremely chummy with a nice and tender-hearted girl.

The girl was interested in photography and always carried a camera with her. She tried to take as many photographs of the boy as possible.

Time passed.

They grew up and drifted apart. He went his way and she went hers.

People change with time, and so the tender-hearted boy grew up to become a hard-hearted man. He became a thoroughly materialistic, flinty and self-centered individual.

Time passed.

He remained a hard-hearted man for a long time. For a long time, he caused misery to a number of people, and—though he would never admit it—was miserable himself.

It came to pass that one day, while casually flipping through the pages of an old book in his library, he came across an old photograph, neatly tucked between the pages of the book. He glanced at the photograph and was about to put it away again when something hit him. For a moment he was startled into immobility. Then slowly, almost apprehensively, he lowered his eyes and looked at the photograph again.

The photograph showed the tearful face of a boy looking at a dead bird in his hand. Something in the face of the boy made him glance away quickly. The man found he could not face the boy he had been.

Then, like a huge tidal wave, his past came flooding over his present, and he found himself floating over a vast ocean of memories— memories of the boy who was, memories of the girl who had taken the photograph, memories of many other things.

He got up and went to the mirror on the wall. He looked at himself for some time. Suddenly, without any warning, a strange sort of bittersweet pain gripped his heart. Like a small child, he burst into tears.

From then on, he was a changed man, a tender-hearted man.

So that is the story. Now what do you think of it?

You think it is nothing but a naive and unrealistic fairy tale?

How stupid of you.

Things like this sometimes (though not often) do happen in the real life.

(Further reading: "A Christmas Carol", by Charles Dickens.)

Chapter 3

Pain tests.

Chapter 4

In the world there are people, though very few, who are brave and noble enough to come forward and offer their help in carrying other people's burden of Pain. When this happens, there is a substantial lessening in the overall amount of Pain in the universe.

Chapter 5

Being sentient is to accept responsibilities. With responsibilities comes Pain. Face it or live the life of an animal.

Chapter 6

Some people maintain that sometimes Pain helps one in better appreciating Pleasure.

(Further reading: "Paingod", by Harlan Ellison.)

Thus ended The Book of Pain.

The distribution of Pain was still not an easy task. The capacity of a creature to bear Pain had to be gauged quantitatively as well as qualitatively. Then the Pain had to be distributed, with justice.

At last, after a lot of deliberation, he started the distribution of Pain. A malady or two here. A misery or two there. Here, the pain of parting from a loved one. There, the pain of an unattained desire. Here, the pain of birth. There, the pain of death. The pain of corporeal punishment here. The pain of self-reproach there... It went on and on and on.

And then the universe was saturated with Pain.

But the task of distributing Pain remained unfinished. There still remained a lot of undispensed Pain in the reservoir.

The dispenser of Pain was stumped.

The time given to him was coming to an end. What should he do now? Unleash extra Pain among the creatures of the universe? No. That was out of question. They would not be able to bear it.

So what was he to do?

And then, going through The Book of Pain again, he found the answer.

Slowly, deliberately, he moved to the pit, bent down, picked up the whole of the surplus Pain and placed this burden squarely upon his own broad shoulders.

He reeled. A darkness descended upon him. He screamed. He wept. Then suddenly, he felt the weight of pain being taken away from him. He sagged to the ground with the intensity of relief.

He slowly opened his watery eyes to find himself surrounded by the gods. Suddenly, the air vibrated with sounds of applause. There, before him, stood a host of gods grinning and cheering him. The Pain had been thrown back into the pit, perhaps for other tests, other times.

One of the gods, the one who had given him The Book of Pain, stepped forward, smiled.

"Welcome to the ranks," he said. "Come, let's go, have a drink." And all the gods, including the new-comer, made their way to the nearest ambrosia parlour.

Wordspell

"For people of my world, places like Ghelenden may be good to visit once in a while, but not to reside in permanently." Believe it or not, I wrote "Wordspell" just for the sake of the above sentence. To know more on the background of Ghelenden, refer to my notes on "Tug of War" elsewhere in this book.

A world named Ghelenden appeared in my life at a time when I was confused and restless.

My name is Jasmina. Call me Jasma. I work as a copywriter for an advertising firm.

That day, it was a few minutes past noon and I was sitting in my cubicle wrestling unsuccessfully with a copy for something called Flit beauty soap, restless and confused.

I was confused because two men had asked me to marry them—Jon and Caleb.

Both of them were my colleagues at the advertising firm. Both of them were young, healthy, and smart. Both were kind, cute and cuddly. In short, I liked them both and had no idea who to choose.

My restlessness had increased to the point of unbearability when there was a knock on the door.

"Come in," I said and the door opened and a strange apparition came in. This apparition was a man, bespectacled, bald pated and bare-foot. He wore nothing but a pair of shorts and an old straw hat. He was of medium height and build and sported a short white beard. He was smoking a pipe. Kindliness and good humor were etched on his face in a network of fine and delicate wrinkles.

"My name is Tim," he said. "I come from a place called Ghelenden and your help is needed in fighting an evil wizard. Will you help us, Jasmina?"

I sat there unresponsive, simply staring at the man, open mouthed.

Tim seemed to find my stupefaction quite amusing. He chuckled.

Suddenly, the ridiculousness of the man's appearance and his proposition hit me and I grinned.

Any other time and I might have simply asked the man to leave my room, sure that he was insane or this was some sort a gag. But then, my restlessness lay heavy upon me and I thought, what the heck, why not go along with the man and see where it all leads?

So I got up and made a slightly mocking bow. "My services are yours," I said. "Lead on, McDuff."

I left the room with him.

Hearing the sound of my footsteps, Jon peered out of his cabin. He gave Tim a startled glance and looked at me questioningly. I shrugged and spread my hands.

"I am going out on some urgent business," I said. "See you later."

Jon nodded and went back to his work.

Outside the office, I turned to Tim.

"Ghelenden, isn't it? To fight a wizard?" I looked critically at my dress. I was wearing a brown and white knee-length frock and a pair of ice-cream white stockings. I had my hair tied in a white scarf and I had cream colored shoes on my feet. Would this dress be suitable for a fight with a wizard, I thought, or should I wear something more appropriate? Perhaps an embroidered robe and a cloak?

"Won't I need any luggage? Clothes, tooth brush, towel?" I asked.

"No. Everything will be provided."

"How do we reach Ghelenden?" I asked. "Riding on a unicorn?"

"No," said Tim. "Riding on thought." And I blinked and found myself standing in an unfamiliar street. Tim stood beside me, pipe in his mouth, his lips curled in a smile.

It was a busy street, lined with shops and houses. People moved about. Everything gave the picture of a street like so many streets in my own city, except for a few minor differences. Not many city streets in our world have a separate lane for unicorns.

I was in Ghelenden.

What have I let myself in for? I had a slight misgiving, which soon vanished in the wonder of it all.

It was a beautiful, bright day here. A playful wind was mussing up the green tresses of tall trees. The sun was bright and made all the things—the buildings, the lamp posts, the trees, the people, the vehicles—cast sharp shadows on the ground.

We were standing in front of a decent looking house, white-walled and red-roofed. A high fence went around it and there was a wooden gate in the fence. The house looked old, quaint, cozy and pleasant.

The gate of the house opened and a young boy of about five came running out of the house and hugged Tim. Tim lifted him up in his arms, kissed him and slowly lowered him to the ground.

The boy was fair, had dark unruly hair, a round, cuddly face. The eyes were big, dreamy and innocent, with intelligence and impishness peering around corners.

Tim noticed my questioning glance.

"His name is Arokyo," he said, "and he is an orphan."

I felt a kinship with Arokyo. I was an orphan too. I lost both of my parents in a car accident before I was seventeen. Good thing that by that time, I was educated enough and world-wise enough to get along all alone with the business of living. Life was not a bed of roses, but I managed respectably well.

The boy, hearing his name mentioned, looked up at Tim and then at me. Hesitantly, he approached me, stared into my face with those soulful eyes, smiled softly and extended his hand to me for a handshake. I smiled, ignored his hand, scooped him up in my arms as Tim had done, and kissed his cheeks. Then I put him down.

Suddenly shy, he ran back the way he had come. Tim followed him and I followed Tim into the house.

The first thing I saw through the gate was a small garden, green with a variety of plants and grasses. The fragrance of freshly watered earth filled my nostrils. Mixed with this fragrance were smells of the myriad flowers that grew all around in wild abandon. In the midst of this splendor, stood the house.

An hour later, after a sumptuous meal followed by tea in the garden, I found myself properly settled in Ghelenden. I found out that we were now in a town called Targot, which was located on the eastern fringe of something called the "Dark Forest," in the land of Ghelenden. Surprisingly, I seemed to be taking everything quite matter-of-factly, as if it was a routine matter for me to be asked to help people in fantastic lands fight their evil wizards.

We sat on wicker chairs, Tim and I, in the garden, chatting together as if we were friends from way back. Arokyo sat on Tim's lap.

"Tell me about yourself," Tim said. "How old are you?"

"Twenty one."

"Today, in your office, you seemed to be utterly lost. Anything in particular troubling you?"

"Jon and Caleb," I blurted out.

Tim settled back in his chair. "Tell me about them."

"Okay. Now how shall I describe Jon? He is slightly slapdash and clumsy. He is extremely witty, caring and full of life when he is with friends, but becomes tongue-tied in the presence of strangers. Usually, his brow is deeply furrowed, as if he is scowling angrily at the whole world.

"Caleb is dapper, suave, soft-spoken. He has one of the most beautiful smiles I have ever seen in a man. He speaks softly and he is always nice with everyone. That is why he is the PR man for our firm."

"That is trouble I can't help you with." Then Tim started telling me about the situation in Targot.

It seemed that a few months back an evil and powerful wizard had moved near Targot. His name was Umrig the Merciless. He had built himself a castle in some place called the Dark Forest, and from there, wreaked havoc on the people of Targot.

"Why me?" I asked. "Why was I selected to fight this wizard?"

"Don't ask me, ask the oracle," said Tim.

"You have an oracle?"

"Yes, and when asked about how to fight Umrig, we were given your name and address."

"Why?"

Tim shrugged. "Why particularly you, I cannot say. But a champion from your world is logical enough," he said, "because Umrig uses evil spells that belong to your world."

"Spells belonging to my world?"

"Yes," said Tim. "I will tell you the names of some of his spells and you will understand."

Some of Umrig's spells were called Socialism, Communism, Economic-policy, Foreign-policy, Party-politics, See-eye-aye, Kay-gee-bee, End-justifies-the-means-and-other-assorted-doctrines.

I nodded. Yes, these were evil spells from my world, right enough.

"Then there are other reasons for your choice," continued Tim. "Umrig's magic is a magic of words. One reason you have been selected is that you are in the advertising business, which depends on word-spells too. Another reason is that you are a woman and only a woman can fight Umrig word for word and come out the winner." I thought of bristling at this statement, but Tim did not give me time. "Further," he continued, "she had to be athletic, a girl who could run fast, jump long. She had to be intelligent, sharp, adventurous and stubborn. I think you were the logical choice."

I reviewed Tim's words. I was athletic, yes, and I could run fast. And of course I was intelligent, and sharp, and adventurous too. But stubborn? Was I stubborn?

"We of Targot desperately need your help," said Tim. "You don't know the misery Umrig is causing. But let me make one thing very clear. Fighting Umrig will not be an easy task. If it was, we would have dealt with him a long time back and would not have required outside help." He puffed on his pipe. "Your path is strewn with danger. Injury and death will dog your footsteps." He paused and gave his pipe another puff. "Knowing all this, do you want to help us? The decision is yours to make. If you say no, it would be perfectly understandable and we will safely return you to your world right now." Another puff on the pipe. "What is your decision?"

"Give me some time to think," I said.

"Okay," Tim said and suddenly smiled and animatedly started chatting with me about this and that. His conversation was so lively that I soon forgot about the decision that I had to make and began having a good time. Tim smiled a lot and he made me smile too. It was fun talking to him.

Sometime during the chat, Arokyo left Tim's lap and came and sat on mine. I kissed him and continued talking to Tim. Slowly, a question began forming at the back of my mind. I had not heard Arokyo's voice even once till now. Why was he such a silent child? I interrupted Tim's flow of talk to ask him this question.

Tim suddenly fell silent.

"Arokyo cannot speak," he said quietly.

I was shaken. Arokyo was dumb?

"A victim of Umrig," continued Tim.

"What?"

"Yes," his voice dropped low. "His parents were killed by Umrig's magic."

"How?"

"Arokyo's parents were farmers. One day, at the time of harvest, Umrig's minions came and demanded one half of the field's harvest as tribute to Umrig. Arokyo's father refused and Umrig does not brook refusal." Tim paused.

"That night," Tim continued, "Umrig himself came to the farmers.

Ahmed A. Khan

Standing by the harvested crops, he waved his hand. Suddenly, something happened to Arokyo's parents. Their faces wild with horror, they got up, lit torches, ran to the crops and set fire to them. The fire spread. It consumed the crops. Then Arokyo's parents threw themselves into the fire. Arokyo was four years old then. He saw all this happen right before his eyes. That was the day that he lost his voice. I found him wandering in the streets of Targot, hungry, dirty and crying."

It took me some time to assimilate all this.

"How do you know this incident in such detail?" I asked in a shaken voice.

Tim thought for a while. He turned to Arokyo.

"Show her," he said.

Arokyo looked at Tim, wide-eyed. Then he turned to me and looked deep into my eyes. Suddenly, the living room and Tim and the daylight all vanished and I was standing beside a burning grain shed. I saw it all, exactly as Tim had described and when I came to, Tim was bending over me in concern. I was screaming.

It was much later that I calmed down.

"What was it?" I asked Tim in a low voice.

"Arokyo is a telepath and can transmit vivid thought pictures to others," he said.

I looked at Arokyo to find his face stained with tears. It made my heart ache.

There was silence for a while, which I broke.

"I will fight Umrig," I informed Tim. In normal circumstances, it would have been funny, a simple, young girl vowing to fight a mighty wizard, but these were not normal circumstances. I was the chosen champion of Targot.

"Thank you, Jasma," said Tim, gently.

I spent that night in Tim's house in Targot.

Early next morning, Tim knocked on the door of my room.

"It is time to go. Get ready," he said and left me.

I quickly finished with my toilet, took a cool, refreshing shower and put on my dress.

Tim was waiting for me at the breakfast table.

"Where is Arokyo?" I asked.

"Still sleeping."

We finished our breakfast in silence. After breakfast, Tim lit his pipe and sat puffing it in silence.

"Your mission begins, lass," he spoke at last. "Let us go."

We went.

There was a horse carriage standing outside the house with two horses hitched to it. Tim clambered up and helped me up beside him. Tim took the reins and we began moving.

We soon left the city behind and turned down a small dusty road.

I do not know how long we traveled. The early morning breeze, the rhythmic clip-clop of the horses' hooves and the steady flow of the carriage on the roads of Targot made me doze off and I woke up only when the carriage stopped.

"Where are we?" I asked.

"At the edge of the Dark Forest," replied Tim.

I looked about. Yes. There was the Dark Forest. If there was any forest that deserved being called Dark, it was this forest. Even in broad daylight, I was unable to see things beyond a few feet from its edge. It was one of the most uninviting places I had ever seen. But due to some strange reason, it fascinated me, exhilarated me.

I left the carriage.

Tim picked up a knapsack from the rear of the carriage and handed it to me.

"It holds some provisions for your journey," he said. "From here on, you will travel alone for I am forbidden to enter the Dark Forest," he said. "Be alert in the Dark Forest. It is a strange place and both good and evil run rampant within it. Your job is to find Umrig and fight him and defeat him any way you can. I wish you good luck." He paused. "Do you have any questions?"

"Yes," I said. "One full day has passed since I left my world. When will I be able to return?" I was thinking of Jon and Caleb and how worried they would be at my absence.

Tim smiled. "Don't you know that in places like Targot time runs at a different rate than the world outside? You can live here even for a year and return to your world within a couple of hours of your time."

I thought over it.

"How will I find Umrig's castle?"

"You will have a guide," he said cryptically. "Any other questions?"

"Yes," I said. "You have told me about Umrig and about Targot's predicament. Now tell me about yourself. What is your involvement in all this? Who are you?"

I saw a peculiar sight. I saw the wrinkled old man blush. Then without answering, he geed up the horses and moved away, leaving me to stare after the vanishing carriage.

I hung the knapsack on my back.

Finally, I entered the Dark Forest, and as I did so, I felt a chill tingle down my spine.

I had hardly walked a few paces when I felt the Dark Forest closing all around me. I felt totally cutoff from the outside. Huge trees and dense underbrush were all around me. Daylight filtered through their thick foliage and spread on the ground in a silvery haze. The ground was lush with soft downy grass.

Wild scents invaded my nostrils. Wild sounds filled my ears.

I do not know how long I walked. In the Dark Forest, time seemed to have lost much of its meaning.

As I continued walking, I realized something. The forest seemed to have distinct pockets of moods. At places it was gloomy. At other places it was quite cheerful.

I began feeling alone and miserable as I wandered aimlessly. Now that I was inside the Dark Forest, what was I supposed to do? How was I to find Umrig? What was I supposed to do after finding him? Where was that guide I was supposed to have?

Suddenly I heard sounds of someone walking through the underbrush. My heart missed a beat. What wild beast would it be? A lion? A tiger? Or would it be some unbelievable monster? A troll? A goblin? I hid behind a tree trunk and waited.

Soon, the creature ambled into view and I gasped at his strange appearance. Imagine a man-like figure, about seven feet tall, extremely thin, every limb and every feature of the face delicate beyond belief. Imagine a certain beauty and gracefulness mixed with the strange and delicate structure just described. Imagine this delicate creature wearing a delicately designed robe of some softly shimmering, green material. If you want description more concrete, even if crude, to sink your teeth into, then imagine a graceful blend of a man and a praying mantis. More than this I cannot say.

Unerringly, the mantis-man approached the tree behind which I was hiding. "Come out. Don't be afraid of me," he said.

His words stung. Afraid? Jasma the fearless?

"So who's afraid," I said in a trembling voice and stepped out.

The mantis-man bowed gracefully. "Welcome to the Dark Forest," he said.

"Who are you?" I asked. My voice was firmer now.

"I am an elf," he said. "I am called Fleigen and I have been sent to guide you to Umrig's castle."

So this was my guide. I breathed a sigh of relief.

"I am Jasmina," I said. "Jasma to friends. Which way for Umrig's castle?"

Fleigen laughed. "Why in such a hurry?" he asked. "First we eat and rest. Come."

"Where to?"

"To my tree house."

I saw Fleigen's tree house.

It was a dream—a dream come true. The tree house was more beautiful than any tree house I could have imagined. The tree on which it was built was probably one of the tallest trees in the Dark Forest. It grew on the banks of a small rivulet called Dreemer. Its foliage was lush green, interspersed with red, blue and yellow flowers which gave off a fragrance slightly similar to musk. Holes were cut in the tree trunk to act as a ladder. We climbed up and up the tree and moved through branches and leaves and more branches and leaves and at last entered the tree house through a trap door fitted into its floor. The tree house was quite spacious. Big windows were cut into all four of its walls. Cloth curtains covered the windows. Looking out of the windows, what one saw, through a network of overhanging leaves and branches, was the blue expanse of the sky and the treetops, in various shades of green, spreading on all sides as far as the eyes could see.

Soon it began growing dark, so Fleigen lit a candle. By the candlelight, Fleigen offered me some food. Whatever it was, the dish looked, smelled and tasted delicious. Then he gave me some fruit juice to drink. It was sweet and refreshing. After the food, I rummaged through my knapsack to see if a nightgown had been packed. I found a pair of pajamas and changed into them while Fleigen stepped out of the trap door for a while. After I had finished changing, I called out and he re-entered. Then, while the night wove its enchantment all around us as it can only be woven in a tree house of an elf in the midst of the Dark

Forest, we chatted.

Fleigen told me a little about himself. He was a young elf, out on his first adventure, and it was an honor being able to assist the champion of Targot. I hope I was modest enough to blush.

Some time in the midst of all our chatting, I dropped off to sleep.

Dawn came. Fleigen woke me up. We put our respective heads out of a window and looked around. Like the night, the dawn too was enchanting. The Dark Forest lay spread before me in a hazy brightness. Dew drops lay thick and heavy on the leaves and flowers of our tree. Standing there high up in a tree house, in the company of an elf, feeling the refreshing morning breezes playing about my face while mists rose out of the treetops, I felt an ache in my heart. I wished I could have my friends, Caleb and Jon, standing there atop the tree house with me at that moment. I wished they could meet this wonderful being, this elf called Fleigen.

We came down the tree house, washed our hands and face in the flowing water of Dreemer and had a breakfast of fruits.

Then it was time to leave.

We started. Fleigen carried a knapsack with him, just like the one I was carrying. After sometime, we came to a small clearing in the forest. In the midst of this clearing was a pool of water.

"This pool will help us in fighting Umrig," said Fleigen.

"How?"

"First, you will have to cut your finger and let a drop of your blood fall in the pool."

"Black magic?" I was alarmed. The only thing I knew about black magic for sure was that it was bad. I also knew that blood was often an important ingredient in black magic.

"No black magic. In fact, no magic at all. In Targot, magic is used only by those who are evil. The drop of blood symbolizes your intention that you are willing to give your blood for your cause. Without this symbol of commitment, the pool will not speak to you."

"Okay, what then?"

"Then certain words will appear on the surface of the water. You must memorize these words for they shall be the key to Umrig's lair."

We approached the pool. The water in the pool was dark and still. I looked around, found a thorn lying on the ground and pricked my finger with it. I let a drop of my blood fall into the pool, then fixed my eyes on the surface of the water. The drop of blood spread as soon as it touched the water, forming a red circle over the dark circle. Within this red circle, words appeared.

These were the words that appeared in the pool: RUN, JUMP, SWIM, CATCH, DUCK.

A few seconds later, the words vanished.

"You got it? You got it all?" the elf asked excitedly.

"Yes," I nodded, "but what in the world am I to do with these words?" And I told him the words.

"For one thing, these words will open the door of Umrig's castle," said Fleigen. "And who knows what other uses they may have."

I had to be satisfied with this.

"What now?"

"Now I will tell you about Umrig's lair and the spells that guard it," said Fleigen, and he proceeded to do so in great detail.

Umrig's castle could not be approached by land. It was too well guarded. The only possible approach could be through the air. This approach was so well protected by strong spells that even birds could not fly over the castle. Of all the creatures in Targot, only a dragon would be powerful enough to pass through these spells.

In brief, Umrig's castle was impregnable. Then what was I doing in Targot?

But Fleigen was full of optimism.

"Don't worry. You will find a solution to the problem of entering Umrig's castle," he said. "After all, you are the champion."

I wished I had his confidence in me.

We moved through the Dark Forest. I was feeling down thinking about Umrig's castle and Umrig himself.

The air suddenly exploded with sounds of breaking branches and falling trees. Unearthly screams tore through the forest air. I turned around, grabbed Fleigen and clung to him in fright. After a few moments, I realized what I was doing. Abashed, I let him go. Targot had gotten itself a really fantastic champion.

"Wh-what is that sound?" I tried covering up my fright.

"It sounds to me like a dragon in pain," he said. "Come, let us look."

A dragon? O dear!

We made our way through the underbrush. We moved closer and

closer to the sounds and at last, the final curtain of the underbrush parted and we were in the presence of a dragon in pain. And it was a presence indeed.

The dragon was at least three hundred feet long from the tip of the nose to the tip of the tail, and about two hundred feet broad from wing tip to wing tip. He was blue and gold. He was flailing and rolling about on the ground and in the process, reducing many of the surrounding trees to splinters. His screams rang through the forest and with each scream, a jet of flame escaped his mouth and nostrils.

"Dragon, hey dragon," shouted Fleigen. The dragon heard his shout and stopped its flailing for a minute to look at us. Our sudden appearance seemed to astonish him. "Huh! Who?" he said.

It did not surprise me that the dragon could talk. I was in Targot, wasn't I?

"We want to help you," Fleigen said. "Tell us what is troubling you."

This statement seemed to further astonish the dragon. These tiny things—an elf and a girl—wanted to help him. It must have amused him to no end. If only he could ignore his pain and laugh.

"Tell us what is wrong with you," the elf shouted again.

Well, there is no harm in telling them, the dragon must have thought.

"I have a sliver of glass in my left eye," he said.

"Oh, oh!" Fleigen was dismayed. "How did you get it?"

"I was climbing the glass mountain and got caught in an avalanche."

"Wait a minute. Aren't we getting our fairy tales mixed up a bit here?" I remarked mildly.

Both of them ignored my remark.

"Oh, you poor thing!" Fleigen exclaimed, addressing the dragon. I looked at him and looked at the three hundred feet long "poor thing." A sliver of glass in the eye? Was it such a big problem? I asked Fleigen.

"For a dragon, it is," said Bel. "Anything falling into the eyes of a dragon cannot be removed unless the dragon can be made to cry so that the tears wash it away."

"I still don't see the difficulty," I said.

"The difficulty is that no amount of pain or sorrow can make a dragon cry."

"Oh, oh!" A perfect Catch-22 situation. Then suddenly I had an idea. "I bet I can make it cry," I said.

"Impossible," was Fleigen's flat reply.

"Let me try," I insisted.

He shrugged. "Why not?" Then he turned to the dragon, who had resumed his flailing and his screaming.

"Hey, dragon," Fleigen hollered. "We can make you cry."

"Don't be ridiculous," said the dragon between screams of agony.

"We really can make you cry," Fleigen assured the dragon.

"Okay, no harm in trying," the dragon agreed.

"But there is something you will have to do first," I said.

"What?"

"You must lie down on your back and you must promise not to move for at least fifteen minutes, no matter what we do to you." I had read in some fairy tale that a promise binds a dragon tighter than any rope. I hoped that was true.

The dragon hesitated, thought it over, and said, "I promise."

The dragon laid himself down on his back. I broke two stout branches from a fallen tree and extended one of them to Fleigen. He looked at me questioningly.

"Tickle him with it," I said and proceeded to tickle the exposed under-belly of the dragon. The dragon started roaring with laughter. Understanding dawned on Fleigen and he enthusiastically joined me and we tickled the dragon and the Dark Forest rocked to the sounds of the dragon's laughter.

"Ha ha ha ha oh ho ha ha ah I say ho please stop ha stop ha I ha ha cannot ho oh ho any more of this ha ha ha," roared the dragon. We went on tickling him. And tears of laughter filled the eyes of the dragon and with the tears, out came the sliver of glass.

"How can I ever repay you puny creatures," the dragon later tried to express his gratitude.

And I had my second brilliant idea of the day.

"You can repay us," I said quickly, "by getting us inside Umrig's castle."

The dragon thought this over.

"Fine," he said, "but the spells protecting Umrig's castle are very strong and I have the power to take only one of you with me through these spells."

Ahmed A. Khan

"I will go," I said, then turned to Fleigen. Fleigen bent down and embraced me. When we broke apart, there were tears in my eyes, and Fleigen's too.

"Take good care of yourself, girl," said Fleigen.

"Take good care of yourself, elf," I said.

I mounted the dragon and took a firm grip on his neck. With a breath-taking whoosh, the dragon took to the air.

We flew over the treetops. There, down below, the Dark Forest lay spread out in brilliant green. Wind screamed past my ears and I held on to the dragon's neck for dear life. My heart was pounding and blood was racing through my veins. I was excited, and I was frightened.

Soon, the treetops opened up to give a view of a castle made of milky white stone. A pale mist and a deathly silence lay over it. We had reached Umrig's castle. A high wall ran around the castle. As the dragon neared the castle, he began to slow down, as if he was encountering some resistance in the air. The dragon pitted his mighty strength against this resistance and broke through it. We had now crossed the castle wall.

The dragon deposited me near the castle door.

"Now you are on your own, tiny," said the dragon. "I go," and he went, and I was on my own, a lonely, frightened girl, standing before the door of a wizard's castle.

Arokyo's tear-stained face swam before my eyes. I clenched my teeth and resolutely stepped up to the castle door. I pushed it to see if it would open. Nothing happened. Then I remembered something. I remembered that the words I had seen in the pool were supposed to open the door to Umrig's castle.

"Run jump swim catch duck," I said.

Slowly, soundlessly, the door opened. It was pitch dark inside. I stepped through the door into the waiting darkness. As soon as I did so, the darkness vanished and an eerie glow filled the air. I observed that I was standing in a huge hall. The door through which I had just stepped in, was now behind me. Ahead of me was an expanse of uncarpeted floor. The floor and the walls of the hall were jet black, as if covered with soot. Far to my right was another door which led to the interior of the castle.

"Welcome to the house of Umrig, Jasmina," a sibilant voice erupted in the hall. I looked about wildly. There was no one to be seen.

The voice laughed softly. "Are you afraid, Jasmina?"

Of course, I was afraid. Who would not be, in my place? But if Umrig was trying to frighten me, he had not reckoned on my stubborn spirit. Suddenly, I was more angry than afraid.

The door far to my right opened and Umrig entered the hall.

Umrig was old. He wore a sleek, black, silky dress. His features were sharp, very sharp. On his head was a hat. In his hand was a cane. In his eyes was sheer murder.

A cold shiver ran down my spine. Here, then, was the man who was terrorizing Targot, the man who had murdered Arokyo's parents.

"You thought that you, a chit of a girl, could defeat me, the great Umrig?" I once again heard his sibilant voice. "Be afraid, for you are going to die for your presumption."

Umrig raised his hand high up in the air and started mouthing some strange words. Slowly, as his voice grew in volume and his flow of words sped up, a ball of fire sprang to existence on the upraised palm of his hand. The ball grew in size. Within moments, it was big enough to engulf me entirely. With a final utterance, Umrig hurled the ball at me.

Watching the fireball float through the air toward me, I almost panicked, but Umrig's taunting "chit of a girl" pierced my panic. I recalled Tim's words: "Umrig's magic is a magic of words. One reason you have been selected is that you are in the advertising business, which depends on wordspells too. Another reason is that you are a woman and only a woman can fight Umrig word for word and come out the winner."

Instinctively, I knew what to do. Mirroring Umrig's earlier gesture, I raised my right hand high up in the air. I had no particular magic spell to utter, but if words were magic, I had them plenty. So I started.

"Flakmaster lipstick," I said, "with its new, fresh mint taste your man is sure to like.

"Ninety percent of the intelligent people of the world use Watergate washing powder."

My voice rang in the hall. Was it wishful thinking or did I actually notice the speed of the fireball reduce? With vigor, I continued my assault of words.

"Want to give instant vertigo to who sees you? Wear our latest psychedelic shirts."

The fireball skidded to a stop ten feet away from me. The intense heat from it was quite painful even at this distance.

"Have you ever seen lightning on four wheels? Go take a peek at the latest model of Mustache, the car that keeps up with the times."

The fireball actually moved back a few feet. Sensing imminent victory, I delivered the coup-de-grace.

"Make him fall all over you. Use Flit beauty soap," I shouted at the top of my voice.

The fireball had had enough. It fled full speed back to Umrig.

Umrig gave a shout of anger and waved his hand in the air. The fireball vanished.

Next, Umrig pulled out a whistle from his pocket and blew on it. Immediately, the hall seemed to be filled with ghouls, demons, trolls, ogres and other strange creatures. They moved menacingly in my direction, led by Umrig.

Could I fight them all off with more words or should I try running away from them? I decided on the later course. I removed my knapsack from my shoulders and threw it away. I dodged the first onslaught and ran like a rabbit to the door on my right.

I emerged into a courtyard and daylight, with Umrig and his minions close at my heels, bellowing angrily. I led them a merry chase down the courtyard, searching frantically for an escape route. The courtyard led to a narrow alley. I sprinted down the alley. Umrig and his entourage followed. The alley suddenly broadened a bit and a deep pit yawned just a few silly millimeters away from my feet. Somehow I managed to stop myself in time before I plunged down the pit.

The palms of my hands went cold and sweaty at the thought of what might have happened if I had not been able to stop my headlong rush. I looked around to see what I had to do now. The pit was wide but did not span the alley from wall to wall. There was a ledge, about a foot wide, on either side of it.

I had two choices. I could either walk the ledge and go to the other side or I could try and jump over the pit. It was a jump of about twelve feet. The clamor of my pursuers was very close and made my decision for me. My heart in my mouth, I took a running jump.

I cleared the pit and before racing ahead, gave a backward glance. The sight I saw made my hands more clammy than ever. I saw the ledges of the pit move into the wall and vanish. The pit now spanned the whole width of the alley.

What if I had taken the ledges instead of jumping over it? I shuddered at the thought.

Umrig and his monsters spotted me. With a roar, Umrig jumped over the pit, closely followed by his scum. I churned my legs faster and faster and managed to put a little distance between us.

The alley ended. I emerged once again into a courtyard. Smack in my path was a huge pond of water.

What should I do now? Should I skirt it or swim across it? What dangers lurked in the water of the pond?

I shall swim, I decided. I could cross the pond swimming underwater. That way, I might be able to dodge my blood-thirsty pursuers.

I removed my shoes and threw them into the pond. Then I dived. Swimming under water, I reached the other side of the pond in less than two minutes.

There were thick reeds growing in the water. Slowly I raised my head a few inches out of the water and peered out from behind the reeds. Umrig had reached the pond and was casting his eyes all around, trying to locate me without success. It looked like I had a moment of rest.

Methodically, I began reviewing my chances of escape. Suddenly, something struck me. Remember the secret words: Run, Jump, Swim, Catch, Duck. Now think over all that had happened to me after coming face to face with Umrig. First I had "run" from his hoard of monsters. Next I had "jumped" over the pit. Next I had "swum" across the pond. And what is more, all these had been the right actions, actions which kept me safe so far. Was this correlation of my actions with the secret words a coincidence? I doubted it.

What now? What was the next word in the series? "Catch".

Catch what? Of course, how about the last word "duck"? Catch duck? Yes.

I looked around. There, right in the middle of the pond was a solitary duck swimming around in short circles.

It sounded like the silliest way of fighting a wrathful wizard but I decided I had to catch that duck.

I went underwater once again and re-emerged very close to the duck. The duck seemed to take no notice of me but it was different with Umrig. He spotted me and gave a shout of pure panic. "There she

Ahmed A. Khan

is. She is going for the duck, the source of all my magic. Stop her."

And the ghouls and demons and ogres and trolls jumped into the pond.

And I stretched my hands and caught the duck.

And the world went topsy-turvy.

There was a crack of thunder and Umrig disintegrated, simply and surely. There was another crack of thunder and Umrig's castle vanished in a cloud of dust and smoke. There were no more cracks of thunder but all the ghouls, demons, ogres, trolls and others ran into the forest, tails between their legs.

The duck in my hand simply vanished.

Dripping wet, I came out of the pond.

"Yoo hoo," I heard a voice filled with joy. It was Fleigen's voice.

I passed out.

I woke up in Tim's house with Tim and Arokyo bending over me, and they were smiling. I smiled back.

Then it was time to leave.

"You know you could live in Ghelenden permanently," said Tim.

I was silent for a minute before replying.

"No," I said. "For people of my world, places like Ghelenden may be good to visit once in a while, but not to reside in permanently."

Tim nodded. "I knew you would say that," he said, "and you are right."

One moment, I was in Tim's house and the next moment I was standing in front of my office, blinking foolishly. I looked at my watch. It said 3.00 PM of the day that I had left for Ghelenden.

Half an hour later, I was in my office, once again struggling with the copy for Flit beauty soap.

Ghelenden had become a pleasant dream.

On the subject of Flit beauty soap, my mind remained a blank for a long time. Then I remembered, as one recalls a dream, the fireball episode with Umrig. The words I had uttered regarding Flit beauty soap came back to me and I grinned with joy. I had the idea for the advertisement.

I picked up my pen and wrote down the copy. Then I wrote down instructions for the illustrator.

The advertisement would show a sly young girl drop a cake of Flit beauty soap in front of a young man. The next panel would show the young man slip over the cake of soap and land into the outstretched arms of the girl. The caption would read: "Make him fall all over you. Use Flit beauty soap."

At least one of my problems of the day was solved. But the other problem remained. I was still confused about whom to marry, Jon or Caleb? But I was the champion of Targot, and knew I would figure it out.

The Maker Myth

The story first appeared circa 2000 in GateWay SF, a magazine now defunct. Later, in 2007, it was featured on the web site of SF Canada and received some excellent comments. Anything else I say about the story will be spoiler.

Something happened. Much that was, and is, was lost in a series of cataclysmic events. The sky darkened for days on end. Then rain came, a deluge that swelled the rivers, the oceans, and washed away the past. And last came the cold. The dark cold. And much that was, was lost completely. Until it could be discovered again.

So it was with great anticipation that people packed the convention hall. Such was the popularity of the guest speaker of the day. There was an air of high expectation all around. The great Mr. Arten was coming here, and he was going to deliver a talk on the origin of life. It was bound to be interesting as he had been working on this subject for several years.

The buzz in the hall suddenly died. The great person had arrived. The audience rose to give him a standing ovation. He bowed and took his seat with great dignity.

First, there were a few speeches by the organizers about the guest speaker, his life and work, his extraordinary contribution to science — in particular his discoveries about the ever-interesting, ever-mystifying subject of the origin of life. The audience fidgeted and murmured, waiting for all these speeches to end and for the great scientist and philosopher to take up the microphone.

Finally, the moment arrived. With ponderous steps, Mr. Arten mounted the podium. He cast a grave glance at the packed hall. A hush fell over the audience.

And then he began speaking. His voice was sonorous, his delivery clear. He exuded an air of supreme self-confidence.

He spoke thus:

Ladies and gentlemen, without beating about the bush, let me say that I am here to prove the creationists wrong.

Let us go about it logically.

What are the arguments that the creationists put forward? The primary one concerns the chain of cause and effect—the argument that the existence of a thing points to the existence of its maker.

Why should this reasoning be true? I agree that we have yet to discover any causeless effect, but does it mean that it does not exist, never did exist and will never exist in the future? As you can see, this line of argument leads us into a labyrinth of philosophical concepts, without helping us reach any conclusive result. We can't prove, beyond all doubt, the truth of this theory. All we can concede is that creationist view is nothing more than a mere hypothesis.

I want to present a counter hypothesis.

Causality does break down at some level of existence, and at that point, a thing can come into existence spontaneously. There doesn't always have to be a maker.

The second argument that the creationists put forward is this: strange objects, pictures and signs have been unearthed which point to the existence, at some time in the very remote past, of the Maker. They believe that at one time, much before our existence, the Maker lived on earth. He created us in order to serve him. But later, something befell the Maker and he vanished from the earth, leaving only vague traces.

Now, this is an interesting argument. I see that my esteemed opponent Mr. Defore is in the audience. I am sure he can provide you with more details about these so called signs of the Maker. However, it was to these very signs that I have applied myself for the past decade. My research has been gathered in a book called "The Maker Myth," which is now undergoing publication. I urge you all to read this book when it comes out. I promise that you will find it interesting and stimulating. In this book, I have taken the alleged signs of the Maker and have postulated possible rational causes for each and every one of them, proving that these signs do not point to a Maker.

So then, if there is no Maker, how did we come into existence? This is the question that I am going to answer now. Listen carefully to the following scenario and see how rational, how intellectually satisfying it is.

In the beginning there was a timeless singularity. This singularity exploded in a big bang and gave birth to two things, matter and energy. The existence of matter and energy resulted in the simultaneous existence of time. The world progressed. Chaos settled into order. The matter, influenced by energy, formed various ordered elements, substances, planets, suns, and so on. One of the planets thus formed was earth.

On earth, several random combinations of elements took place and several substances were formed. Of these substances was also the substance of our bodies. This substance, when formed, had no coherent shape. Then, with the passing of eons and the continuation of random combinations, once again order resulted from chaos and some of the substances arranged themselves into an orderly shape—the shape of our bodies. The substance was of course, lifeless. It probably lay lifeless for several more eons until, on pure chance, a bolt of lightning hit it. Electricity coursed through it, and this electricity did strange things to it. It gave sentience and motion to the substance.

That was the first being, the father of us all. Once he became alive, he took control of what so far had been a random process. He began gathering and giving shape to the substances. He discovered how to create electricity and he also discovered other sources of power. With these power sources, he gave life to the images he had assembled. In short, he created more beings like himself, who then helped him to create still more, till the world was populated by our like.

That is my hypothesis about our origin. Tell me honestly. Isn't it a beauty? And where does the so-called Maker come into it? He doesn't.

In conclusion, ladies and gentlemen, I firmly believe that us robots came into being by ourselves as I have described, and the myth of Man, the Maker, is just that—a myth.

Traveler From An Antique Land

This story started with a challenge. I kept hearing that the time-travel trope had been explored inside out and nothing new could be said about it. I agreed with one thing: the time-travel paradox stories were old hat even before my birth. So then the first question was: How? How can one travel in time without the possibility of paradoxes? The second question was: Why? Why would someone do it? The third question was: Who? Who is the time-traveling person? Actually, the third question became the most fascinating one because I picked a real-life person as my time-traveler and managed to answer a few unanswered questions about his life.

This story is being published here for the first time.

Was he a madman, a consummate actor and prankster taking advantage of the similarity of facial features, or truly the person he claimed to be? To this day, I do not know for sure, but as a result of that encounter, I had the makings of my first book.

I had just finished my first term at the university where I was researching for my thesis on lost mysteries. Lost ships. Lost planes. Lost people. There is always a compelling story in such mysteries.

I was home on a week's holiday. My home was in a quiet countryside where the neighbors are few and far between. One evening, I was sitting on an outcropped rock beside the dirt road close to my house and I was reading "The Devil's Dictionary" for research purposes, when I noticed someone coming down the road towards me.

He stopped wearily and looked at me silently for some time before asking, "Would you mind if I sit here with you for a while?"

I looked at him carefully. I consider myself a pretty good face reader and this is what I guessed about him from his face: sharp, cynical and yet kindly, not given to pampering fools. He sported a distinctive moustache and a short beard; he was quite handsome and had a good tan as though he had been out in the sun for some time. I supposed he was in his sixties, though I found out later I was being overly generous. He looked tired, as though he had been walking a long time.

He wore brown trousers, a brown safari jacket and a panama hat and carried knapsack on his back, all of which looked quite old and worn.

"Not at all," I replied.

He sat down beside me on the rock and there was silence for a while as he stared out at the quiet countryside.

"Good to see that book is still around and still being read," he said, pointing to The Devil's Dictionary. "You must be an intelligent young man to be reading it." He had a strange smile on his face, as if he knew something that I did not.

"Thank you," I said, for the want of anything better to say.

"My name is Herbert," I said, extending my hand.

"Ambrose," he grasped my hand.

He removed his hat. His hair were receding in the middle. Something in his looks nagged at me.

"New to this place?" I asked.

"Yes."

"Looks like you've been traveling a lot."

"You don't know how much."

"What do you do?"

"Once I was a writer. Now I am a traveler."

I looked at his knapsack. "Traveling salesman of some kind?"

"No. I am a time traveler."

"What?"

"You don't believe me."

"Of course, I don't."

He gave me that enigmatic smile again. "Just for fun, assume that I am telling the truth. What questions, if any, would you ask me then?"

I thought it over. This could be fun. Whatever he was, I was interested.

"Okay, first question. How do you know our language so well? Is it spoken in your time too?"

"Yes," he said. "I am not that much removed from your time."

"Does that mean time travel is just around the corner?" I asked.

He did not respond, but he looked amused.

Then I asked him, "Tell me something about your times."

"Hmm?" He fell into a reverie, a sad smile playing over his lips. "Those were quite good times, you know," he said at length, rather wistfully. "Not all good. My two sons died and my wife was unfaithful. I had a daughter too. Someday, I hope to locate her."

"What year do you come from? How far ahead in our future?" He turned and looked at me in a strange way.

"You don't understand," he said gently. "Time-travel to the past involves paradoxes out of man's control."

"I know. Science fiction is full of them."

"And because of these paradoxes," he continued, ignoring my interruption, "time-travel to the past is out of reach of common man within the boundaries of the normal universe."

Comprehension did not come immediately. "But—but that means..."

"Yes, I think you understand now. I come not from your future, but from your past."

I assimilated this information. A thousand questions raised their heads in my mind. "Time-travel was known in the past?" I was starting to take this man seriously.

"Yes."

"Then why is it not known today?"

"Even in those days, time travel was known only to a select few. With time, and wars and disasters, men lost the knowledge of time travel among other things."

"What other things?"

"Values, for one."

At that time, I thought it was a corny statement. At that time I was young.

Shading his eyes with his hand, he looked at the burning orb in the sky. "I have very short time before my next jump," he said. "Already, the time to leave is drawing near."

"You are going back?" That made me think. "Wait a minute. Didn't you say that traveling back in time is not possible?"

"Yes."

"But if you are going back to your time from here, it means you are traveling to the past."

He smiled, and there was something both mocking and sad about his smile. "Whatever gave you the idea that I was going back to my time? No, my friend. I am jumping forward some twenty years in your future."

"Why?"

"Why what?"

"Why have you left your time? What made you undertake this one-way super fast journey into the future? What is the purpose?"

This time, he was silent for quite a while. It seemed as if he was finding it difficult to give words to his thoughts. At last, he spoke.

"I have to leave you soon, so I will try to tell you about it as briefly as I can.

"In my time, a great scientist studied the sun. He found out that the

Ahmed A. Khan

sun was cooling down at an incredible rate. If this cooling rate went unchecked, we would have a dead sun on our hands within a few centuries or so." He paused and I pounced.

"Several decades ago, some scientists believed that stars cooled down with time. But later discoveries about the evolution of stars proved this wrong. Stars don't cool down." You see, I knew my astronomy even though I was not a science student.

He looked at me with what I thought was a grudging respect.

"Perhaps," he said. "But our sun turned out to be an anomaly. It was really cooling down."

"Who was this scientist and how far back was this?"

"That was in the early twentieth century and you would not recognize the name of the scientist. He was a recluse, living in a small village near Chihuahua in Mexico. Now don't interrupt. I don't have much time left.

"Some of the greatest minds of our times came to a decision. There was one way to prolong the life of the sun. First of all, a tremendous source of energy was needed. We knew that time travel to the future was accompanied by the release of a great quantity of energy. The only problem was how to channel this energy to the sun. Once this problem was solved, there was a call for volunteers. Of those who volunteered, I was selected. So here I am. With every jump into the future, there is a release of energy and this energy is siphoned off to the heart of the sun by a small device I carry with me. Here, let me show you." He undid the top buttons of his shirt and pulled out a chain that hung around his neck. Attached to the chain was what looked like a metal ball with strange markings on it. I looked at it, silently.

He turned the gadget around in his hand. "Round," he said, "like time itself."

"Isn't it dangerous, your showing this device so openly to strangers? Someone may try to grab it from you."

He smiled. "I don't show it to everyone. Neither do I tell everyone my story. I like you, particularly seeing that you have good taste in literature." He pointed to the book in my hand.

"So when did you make your first jump?"

"It was in the December of 1913. Mexico was in turmoil and Pancho Villa was busy capturing Ojinaga.

"I have left my times, my world, my friends, never to return to them, ever moving onwards, with no time to call my own, no home to look forward to. I have sacrificed a lot to prolong life on this planet."

"Where do you expect this to end?"

"At my death or at the time of the big crunch, if it is not very far off in the future."

He paused, then said, "Farewell, my friend of a few moments. It was nice meeting you and talking to you. I find you intelligent and sensible and I think I can count you among those people who perhaps will not disappoint me. I may see you, or hear of you again, in twenty years. God be with you." He got up and started walking down the road.

Just then I looked down at the book in my hand. The back cover was facing me and it had a photo of the writer. I realized that this was the source of my sense of familiarity with the traveler. He looked quite like the writer in the photo, except that the writer did not have the rugged beard.

Suddenly, all those bits and pieces of information that he had given me came together in my mind. He was a writer and was pleased that I was reading The Devil's Dictionary. Then there were the sad details of his family history and he was in Mexico in 1913.

"Wait," I shouted. "Are you Ambrose Bierce?"

He turned, gave me a nod, and then vanished into the sunset.

The Presonic Man

This is my absolute favorite story. This is also one of my most reprint-ed stories. It was first published in Anotherealm way back in 1998. Then it was reprinted in GateWay S-F, Antipodean (where it stood #1 in a readers' poll) and at Ragged Edge. The story was also translated into Lithuanian and Croatian, and published in "Spin" and "Dorados Raganos," respectively.

It was a bright spring morning when James Anders' life changed.

James was a moderately well-to-do writer. He had no living relatives and lived alone in his apartment.

That morning, he switched on the TV. It was a cartoon, but the sound he heard was not the sound of a cartoon, but of news being read. Was something wrong with the TV?

Had two channels somehow gotten mixed up? Then he heard the news reader announce the date. He sat bolt-upright. How could it be the 25th of May, today? Yesterday, when he had gone to sleep, it had been the 20th. What was going on? Had he slept for four days—a modern day Rip Van Winkle? He ran outside, picked up the newspaper lying on his doorstep and looked at the date. Twenty first of May.

He had not slept for four days.

That was just the beginning. That whole day, he kept hearing voices: voices of his friends, his neighbors, the voice of Jenny, and his own voice. What was going on? Was he going mad? But there was no insanity in the voices he heard.

He thought hard, struggling against a rising sense of panic. Slowly, almost shyly, a tiny idea raised its head. He had a hypothesis. It was fantastic. Nevertheless, he decided to test it.

Next morning, he switched on the television. Once again, the picture on the tube did not match the sounds. He heard the date being announced, and it was the twenty sixth of May. Hypothesis proved!

No matter how fantastic, it was probably true. His sense of hearing had extended four days and a couple of hours into the future.

First, he went into panic. Then, recovering, he quietly sat at his writing table for hours, mentally working out the ramifications of his condition. There were various things, big and small, to take care of. For instance, if someone rang the doorbell, he would not hear it. He had to have some kind of visual indication for it. Then there was the phone. This was one instrument that would become almost totally useless to him. And what about conversation with people? He could talk to them and they would hear him, but when they talked, he would have heard it four days ago. How then to have a coherent conversation? The only solution was to tell everyone that he had gone totally deaf. Let them communicate with him via writing.

And life went on with all its strangeness.

His pre-sonic condition had its advantages. He made it a habit of hearing the business news bulletins on the TV, and armed with advance knowledge of the market, he started playing the stocks. Inevitably, his income became healthier and healthier. In turn, he became quite a philanthropist and had no end of fun.

No one knew about his abnormality till he heard himself telling Jenny about it—Jenny who reminded him of paddy fields and milk and honey and everything that is fresh and wholesome—and did not hear Jenny scream or panic. So four days later, he did tell her about it, and she, after a brief adjustment period, accepted it and said so in writing.

And one day, he heard himself asking Jenny to marry him. So naturally, four days later, he did ask Jenny to marry him and Jenny accepted, and they did become man and wife and lived happily for quite some time...

...till the time that he heard Jenny crying with grief. And this grief was over his death.

He immediately got busy straightening out his things, preparing his will, loving and cherishing Jenny.

The next day, he heard his friends come to bury him.

And then his world went dead silent for some time.

And then he heard a terrible voice say: "Who is your God?"

And he had three days to find the correct answer to that question.

Tug of War

A long time ago, in 1990, while working in Kuwait, I created a fantasy world called Ghelenden as part of a simple RPG game I designed exclusively for my kids to play. Ghelenden's hub is the Dark Forest which is the source of all that is fantastic in this world.

Several countries border the Dark Forest, each with its peculiarities, cultures and creatures. This world had magic but what differentiated it from other fantasy worlds was that only the evil had recourse to it. I had hardly finished designing the game when something happened and I lost all files on my computer. I did not have the energy to rewrite the game but I did write five stories set in this world, two of which are included in this collection. This is one of them and the other is "Wordspell."

I love stories that have a physically weak protagonist facing a physically strong antagonist and coming out the winner through the exercise of ingenuity. Examples of stories in this category that I have loved are Monument (Lloyd Biggles, Jr.), Dune (Frank Herbert), the Foundation stories (Asimov), and the Dorsai stories (Gordon Dickson).

If you look at that list, you will note that not one of them is a fantasy. Well, "Tug of War" is.

On the White Mountain, surrounded by the great Dark Forest, stood the beautiful Palace of Dawn, the ancestral home of Bel, the wisest person in Ghelenden.

In the Palace of Dawn a young man and a young woman stared out of their bedroom window, their eyes taking in the awesome beauty and grandeur of the Dark Forest and things beyond.

What they saw beyond worried them.

"How accurate is your news of this impending attack on Jolania?" asked Bel, the young woman.

"Very accurate," replied Bo, the young man.

"What of the young prince? You know him quite well."

"Actually, it is a good thing that King Corill is ill and Prince Nilcar is sitting on the throne. He will be a better leader than his father. More open-minded at the least."

"But he will need our help in order for Jolania to survive."

"He will—and he will have it, whether he likes it or not."

Bel sighed. "It looks like our honeymoon must end."

* * *

On the western fringe of the great Dark Forest, there was a small kingdom called Jolania.

Jolania had been a peaceful kingdom until the day the news came that the neighboring kingdom of Cirambar was planning to attack Jolania.

Prince Nilcar was extremely worried. He knew that between Cirambar and Jolania, Jolania was much weaker militarily and could never stand the onslaught of Cirambar.

Young Prince Nilcar called a meeting of his ministers to discuss the situation and to try and find a possible way to save his country.

The ministers pondered for hours, and for hours they hemmed and hawed, but no one could come up with a useful solution—none, that is, until Bo, the youngest of the ministers, suggested that the prince should solicit the help of the wisest person in Ghelenden.

"Who is this person?" asked Nilcar.

"Her name is Bel," said Bo.

"Her? It's a woman?"

"Yes."

Nilcar thought over the matter. Seeing no other alternative, he decided there was no harm in at least consulting this lady about the problem.

"Get her," he ordered.

"Begging your pardon, my prince," said Bo. "Bel requires that whoever is seeking her help should come to her personally."

The prince was indignant.

"That's ridiculous," he said. "Me, go to some witch woman and seek her aid?"

"First," said Bo, "she is not a witch. And second, you need her and she does not need you."

The other ministers gasped at Bo's audacity, but prince Nilcar saw the logic behind it. Bo was happy that he had not been wrong in his good opinion of Nilcar.

"How do I go about seeing this woman?" he asked.

"It is a secret and I would like to tell you about it in privacy," said Bo.

The prince raised his eyebrows, half in question and half in mild amusement. Then he ordered his other ministers to leave, which they did grudgingly.

Once they had left, Bo said, "To find Bel you have to go to the Lagren mountain. At the foot of the mountain, there is a small village. In this village is a restaurant, the only one in the place. You have to go to this restaurant and tell the owner that you want to see Bel. Then, the next day, sharp at sunrise, you have to wait for Bel outside the village."

"Why such elaborate procedure?" asked Nilcar.

"Precautionary measures. Bel has a lot of enemies."

"She has a lot of secrets, huh?"

"Yes."

Ahmed A. Khan

"How do you know so much about her?"

"That's a secret too," said Bo.

That might be true, but this talk between the prince and Bo was a secret no longer. A canny and carefully hidden pair of ears had heard the dialogue and a mouth was itching to repeat it to someone who would pay well for the information.

* * *

The next day, the rising sun found Nilcar waiting for Bel at the foot of the Lagren mountain. The mountain air was invigorating in spite of being quite cold.

Ivory dragons are rare and legendary creatures. The old books say that some ivory dragons are shape-changers. It would be a strange and beautiful sight to see such a dragon—smaller and infinitely more graceful than a regular dragon—soaring on its pearly wings through the sky.

Against the backdrop of the dark mountain and the expanse of the sky in the pale light of dawn, the sight seemed more strange than ever, more beautiful than ever. The dragon flew so silently that Nilcar was not aware of its presence till it was almost upon him. The dragon was pearly white and carried on its back the most attractive girl Nilcar had ever seen. She was young, vibrant, fair, and dressed in a loose, gray hooded robe tied at her waist with a black sash and had long white boots on her feet. The girl looked steadily at him even as her dragon came to rest close to where he was standing. The rising sun, which was behind them, seemed to cast a golden lining around their silhouette.

The tableau remained fixed for quite a while. At last, it was the girl who broke it.

"Well?" she said.

Nilcar closed his mouth with a snap and then tried to say something. It came out as a gurgle.

The girl gave Nilcar a few more minutes to gather himself. Then once again she broke the silence.

"Alright, what do you want from me?"

"Me? Want? Wh-who are you?" stammered Nilcar.

"I am the one whom you wanted to meet," said the girl with elaborate patience. "Now tell me what you require."

"You!" gasped the prince. "You are Bel?"

"Yes."

"But, I thought—"

"That I would be an old crone and would come to you riding on a broomstick." Bel completed his thought with a smile.

"I.."

Before Nilcar could finish, half a dozen men, naked swords in their hands, leapt out from behind some nearby rocks and fell on them. Just then, Nilcar heard a sound which he would always remember with awe. It was the sound of an ivory dragon in anger. And then everything began happening very fast.

Bel drew her sword and jumped off the dragon. The dragon wheeled. The peace of the morning was shattered into a thousand shreds by a sudden cacophony of clashes, clangs, swishes and screams. Bel swung her sword and killed the nearest attacker. The dragon's claws tore one man and its teeth bit another into two.

Nilcar, before he knew what was happening, found himself beset by two attackers. His well-honed reflexes saved him as, in a single, swift motion, he drew his sword and ran it through one of them. The second man would probably have drawn blood, but before he could hit Nilcar, he fell flat on his face with Bel's sword sticking out of his back. The last of the attackers, seeing the fate of his comrades, began to run. Without hesitating, Bel pulled her sword out of the dead man's body and threw it. It flew gracefully through the air and pierced the fleeing target with uncanny accuracy. Bel walked up to the fallen man and pulled her sword out of his body. She picked up some sand from the ground and with it, started rubbing the blood off her sword.

"Now tell me why you wanted to see me?" Bel once again addressed Nilcar.

Nilcar was taken aback. Bel was treating the incident as if it was perfectly normal, as if killing half a dozen people was her regular chore before breakfast.

And the dragon. Such a beautiful creature, and so awesome in a fight.

"What was all this about?" Nilcar asked, as he viewed the six bodies lying on the ground.

"My enemies, obviously," said Bel. "Looks like I will have to devise a new route of contact now. The village restaurant route is a secret

Ahmed A. Khan

no longer."

"But they attacked me too."

"You were an added bonus," she said. "And now," she continued, turning to Nilcar and stopping him from asking her any more questions about her affairs. "We do not have time to waste. Why did you want to see me?"

"In what way can you help me?"

"In what way do you want me to help you?"

"I don't know."

"Neither do I," Bel said. "But since you have gone to the bother of coming all the way here looking for me, you might as well tell me your problem."

"What good would that do?"

"Maybe nothing."

"Are you the same Bel who had defeated the tyrant Sral?"

Bel glanced at the dragon, and the dragon turned its head and met her eyes. The prince saw this interchange and was more than a little nonplussed. What a mysterious girl! What a mysterious dragon!

Bel turned back to the prince but did not say anything. She only smiled.

"Are you really ..." the prince hesitated.

"The wisest person in Ghelenden?" Bel completed his sentence for him. "People say so, but I have my doubts," Bel's voice was dry. "Now, are you going to state your problem or do I say goodbye?"

"Are you aware of our situation?" the prince asked.

"Yes."

"Then you must know what I want to consult you about."

"You want to know how to face the impending assault on Jolania."

"Yes."

"What's the problem?"

"The problem is that Jolania is very weak compared to Cirambar."

"In ancient books on fighting tactics, there is a standard method for dealing with such situations."

"What?"

"Throw the enemy off-balance."

"How?"

"By doing something totally unexpected."

"I don't understand."

"Let me illustrate it for you. Between you and me, which of us do you think is stronger physically?"

"After seeing you fight just a few minutes ago, I am not sure, but alright, I would say that I am stronger than you."

Bel removed the sash from her waist. Then, at her instructions, he held one end of the sash as she held the other.

"Now suppose we have a tug-of-war. Who do you think will win?" She asked.

"I would think I have more chance of winning," said the prince cautiously.

"Alright, pull."

They began pulling at the sash. Surprisingly, Bel was much stronger than Nilcar had imagined. He increased his effort and immediately knew that he would win because he was stronger. Then suddenly Bel let go of the sash and the next instant, he found himself sprawling on the ground.

"That is what I mean by unbalancing the enemy," said Bel.

* * *

Warlord Menin of Cirambar was forty and full of energy. Everything had been rosy for him from the time that old king Dekon of Cirambar had died and prince Ronar had been crowned the new king.

King Dekon had not only been a shrewd ruler, but he had been an excellent military commander too. While he lived, General Menin could never outshine him and so, in his own opinion, could never amount to anything significant in history. But now it was different. King Ronar was blood-thirsty but not brave, cunning but no military tactician. Further, he was greedy, power-hungry and much given to wine and wenching. In short, he was just the sort of king under whose reign, Menin could flourish. And, who knew, there might come a time when he would be more than a warlord. It was a sweet thought, and something to look forward to.

The attack on Jolania had been Menin's idea. The power and influence of a warlord depended on wars. And for a long time, there had been no significant wars in Ghelenden.

Jolania was famous for the beauty of its womenfolk and for its diamonds. Gershner valley in Jolania was the largest source of diamonds

Ahmed A. Khan

in the whole of Ghelenden. These facts, and the fact that Cirambar was militarily more powerful than Jolania, had made king Ronar readily agree to General Menin's proposal.

So now, warlord Menin, with his army of five thousand well-armed soldiers, was ready to make his way to Jolania. He was also thinking, in increasingly sweet anticipation, about the dames and diamonds of Jolania.

The first defensive line of Jolania was the border town of Lakinia, which was just a week's march from Cirambar.

* * *

In Jolania, strange things had begun to happen. Under orders of prince Nilcar, his most trusted henchmen went from town to town, house to house, searching for and confiscating any and all sorts of arms and weapons from the people. The rumor was that Nilcar had gotten the idea that the people of Jolania were turning against him and were planning a revolt. The news of this unrest in Jolania reached Cirambar and made General Menin very happy. The conquest of Jolania would be much easier than he had imagined.

The arms confiscated from the gentry by Nilcar's men were secretly taken to Lakinia and hidden in a dungeon. As days went by, this collection of arms grew to monumental proportions.

A large collection of diamonds and other such riches were also gathered together and hidden in another dungeon of Lakinia.

Hundreds of prostitutes from various towns in Jolania were contacted, and under threats of death and promises of riches, were thoroughly coached in their future duties. They were ordered to infiltrate lakinia. Most of the Lakinian women were spirited out of Lakinia and their places taken up by the infiltrating prostitutes.

A number of criminals under death sentences were taken out of their jails and sent to Lakinia, where they were dressed in the uniforms of the Jolanian army.

Lastly, prince Nilcar went to Lakinia under disguise.

Lakinia was ready and waiting.

* * *

The army of Cirambar was a day's march from Lakinia and had made camp when, in the dead of night, a horseman approached..

The soldiers guarding the camp drew their swords. "Stop!" they said. He stopped, got down from the horse and approached the soldiers, arms held wide, showing that he was unarmed and meant no harm.

"I have come to see the warlord," declared the man. "I have important news for him."

"Who are you?" asked the guard.

"Please, let me see the warlord. It is very important."

Under the light of the camp fires, the soldiers looked carefully at the man. He was young, but from his dress and bearing, appeared to be an important man.

"Wait here," said one soldier and, while the other soldiers kept a close watch on the man, he went to the tent of the warlord and entered it. He returned soon with permission for the man to be sent to the warlord.

The man was thoroughly searched for any concealed weapons. Satisfied, the soldiers allowed him to enter the tent of the warlord.

The man went and stood respectfully before the warlord.

Menin looked the man up and down. "Who are you and what do you want?" he asked.

"I am the mayor of Lakinia and I have come to ask for your help and to offer you our help in return," the man said.

"What?" Menin was taken aback.

"As you surely know, our king is seriously ill and the affairs of the kingdom are being looked after by prince Nilcar. The people of Jolania are not happy with prince Nilcar and are willing to help you in capturing Jolania."

"Well, well, this is something," Menin said.

"I, on behalf of the citizens of Lakinia, can promise you that tomorrow, when you approach our town, you will find our doors open to you and your army. We already destroyed Lakinia's garrison."

"Well, well," repeated Menin. Things were moving too fast for him.

* * *

The next day, it happened exactly as the mayor of Lakinia had promised.

Menin and his army marched into Lakinia unhindered and were hailed by the populace as conquerors and deliverers from the tyranny of prince Nilcar. On the streets of Lakinia lay a few bloody corpses in Jolanian army uniforms. This must have been Nilcar's garrison, thought Menin.

Soon, the conquering army was well stationed in Lakinia. The mayor was proving more than helpful in every way. The soldiers of Cirambar were treated as heroes and were supplied with quite a few luxuries. Drinks were plentiful and at night, the prostitutes, in the disguise of respectable Lakinian women, moved among the soldiers, offering their services to them, as if in hero worship. The Cirambarians never had it better.

Three days passed like lightning. On the third day, Menin decided to move ahead to the next Jolanian town, but the ever helpful mayor offered him something that he could not very well pass by. It seemed that one of Nilcar's soldiers, under torture, had informed the mayor that a huge stock of weaponry lay hidden in the dungeons of Lakinia.

The mayor took Menin to the spot which he said had been indicated by the soldier under torture. Menin's eyes popped when he saw the huge hoard of weapons. These seemed to be his lucky days.

Four days went by in taking stock of the weapons and shifting them to a proper storing place.

On the seventh day of the arrival of the Cirambarian army in Lakinia—and when Menin was once again getting restless—the mayor, who had now become a close friend of Menin, came to him and revealed yet another secret. Another of Nilcar's army officials, also under torture, seemed to have revealed the existence of untold treasure in another part of the dungeons of Lakinia.

These seemed to be eye-popping days for Menin. The warlord just could not believe his luck at the sight of the immense treasure. If this was the beginning, imagine what the rest of Jolania would have in store for him. He immediately took the treasure under his wing.

Ronar received the news of Menin's successes. He received the news of the weapons, the wealth and the popularity Menin seemed to have acquired in Lakinia. Ronar, knowing Menin's ambitious nature, started becoming apprehensive. He sent Menin a message ordering him to gather the loot and return to Cirambar.

Return? When every step that Menin took led him from success to success? So Menin sent back a very diplomatic message, praising Ronar to high heavens and promising him more wealth and power than he could dream of, if Ronar only gave Menin the go-ahead for the complete conquest of Jolania.

This was just a delaying tactic. Menin knew that, in actual fact, he was disobeying his king and so committing treason, but in his new found power of weapons, wealth and, as he supposed, men of Jolania, he was not much bothered with the thought. In fact, fates seemed bent on leading him directly to the throne of Jolania. Once there, who could tell what other vistas and roads would open for him. He would not be a mere army warlord for long, and Ronar could go to hell.

Thoroughly alarmed at Menin's noncompliance with his orders, Ronar declared him a traitor, gathered an army of ten thousand men, and immediately set out for Lakinia to crush him.

Hearing of this, Menin began preparations to fight Ronar. The mayor advised him to send the womenfolk out of Lakinia for the duration of the fight so that the soldiers would have no diversions and would be on full alert. Menin agreed. Meanwhile, the mayor promised him full support. The men of Lakinia would join Menin's army in fighting Ronar.

That day, the prostitutes began leaving Lakinia in groups. With the prostitutes, hidden in various ways, the citizens of Lakinia also moved out of Lakinia.

The next day, late in the evening, Ronar's army reached the walls of Lakinia and laid siege.

That night, the mayor casually walked up to the place where Menin had stored the hoard of weapons. As he neared the Cirambarian soldiers who were guarding the weapons, he gave a soft whistle and an ivory dragon and a girl holding a naked sword stepped out of the darkness of the night. The mayor immediately drew his sword and then the three of them calmly killed the thoroughly startled and unprepared soldiers before they could even wonder what was happening.

This done, while the mayor and the girl wiped and sheathed their swords, the dragon opened its mouth wide. Flames sprang out of his mouth and spread over the weapons. In less than two heart-beats, the weapon heaps had become piles of slag and cinder.

"Too bad we cannot do anything about the treasure we gave Menin," the mayor said regretfully.

"Yes, too bad, but I don't think the treasure will do Menin or Ronar much good," said the girl.

The girl then mounted the dragon and beckoned to him. The mayor hesitated. "Can the dragon carry both of us?"

Bel smiled. "He is stronger than he looks."

That night, the warlord Menin of Cirambar saw an incredible sight. He saw an ivory dragon flying very low. The dragon had two riders. One was a girl and the other was the mayor of Lakinia, who, looking down and spying Menin, waved cheerfully before the dragon soared away into the night sky.

Before Menin could wonder what was going on, he saw some soldiers running toward him. As if in a dream, or rather a nightmare, he saw their lips move and he heard them inform him of the destruction of the hoard of weapons.

With the ego-deflating and heart-sinking sensation of having been had thoroughly, Menin marshalled his army and fell back to the serious business of fighting Ronar.

* * *

"Looks like your plan was successful," said the mayor of Lakinia, who was of course prince Nilcar in disguise.

"Yes," said Bel. " Now, they will fight each other, and the fight will weaken them both, and so they will no longer remain a threat to Jolania."

"Not bad, even considering the sacrifice of a lot of wealth and of Lakinia," said Nilcar in a well-satisfied tone.

"Thank you for everything you did, Bel," said the prince after a while.

"What for?" said Bel. "You did most of the work."

"Yes, but the plan was yours. And at the end, you and your dragon gave active help too, in destroying the weapons and spiriting me away from Lakinia."

The king's palace was in sight and the dragon descended. Prince Nilcar clambered off. Nilcar and Bel waved each other goodbye, and the dragon spread its wings preparing to take to the skies when Nilcar suddenly called.

"Bel."

"Yes," Bel turned.

"Will you marry me?"

The dragon gave Bel an amused wink, which passed unnoticed by the prince.

Bel gave him an extremely friendly smile. "No," she said as kindly and as affectionately as possible. "I am already married." Then Bel and the dragon were gone.

* * *

The dragon flew Bel to the fantastically beautiful Palace of Dawn. Inside the palace, the shape of the dragon began to alter and change in slow, graceful steps, until in the place of the dragon, there stood a naked, handsome, long-haired and bearded young man.

The man grabbed for a dress which lay at hand, but grinning, Bel snatched the dress away.

"Give me my dress, you shameless wench," said the young man and grabbed at Bel, who nimbly evaded him and ran on. Laughing, the naked young man gave chase.

Things took their natural course from thereon, and soon they found themselves on the bed, and no longer was the young man alone in his nakedness.

When things had quieted down, they lay on the bed, close and cozy.

"The nerve of that princeling!" said the young man, with mock indignation. "Proposing to my wife right before my eyes."

Bel laughed. "How could he know that the dragon was not just a dragon but something very special?" she said. "By the way, he sure is an attractive young man."

"Hey! Hey! Careful there, or you will find me out there chasing virgins."

"That is what unicorns are supposed to do, not dragons."

"Who cares!"

Bel laughed.

"Congratulations on the success of your plan," she said.

"Our plan," corrected the young man. "It turned out really well, didn't it?"

Ahmed A. Khan

"The threat of Cirambar has been taken care of," he continued. "And you have made quite an impression on Nilcar who will soon become king. By the way, I think he is a good one. Happy? You now have enough clout to influence his future kingly decisions in the right direction for the future of the country."

"And don't forget about your own enhanced influence over Nilcar, Bo dear."

The young man called Bo, who had been a dragon a short while ago, smiled.

"I would rather enhance my influence over you," he said, and proceeded to do so.

Angels

A science fiction murder mystery/courtroom drama. This story underwent several revisions and improved immensely under the able guidance of Seth Crossman, the editor of this collection.

Rachel woke early with the feeling that she was missing something. This case seemed impossible to win.

She lay in bed listening to Robert breathe. She turned to admire him. The soft whoosh of his breath, the slight rise of his chest, his brown hair, curled at the tips, his perfect skin and rugged chin. He was perfect. Oh, so perfect! He was an angel, pure and simple. And he loved her. She wore proof of that. She played with the wedding ring as often as she held it up to the light to admire the sparkle. She had only been wearing it for three weeks, but it felt right. How could she be so lucky?

Then she saw him staring at her. The clarity of his blue eyes, the fond love in them took her breath away. She ducked her head shyly, a soft smile coming unbidden to her lips. What was he thinking? How could he love a woman like her? Men always seemed to think she was beautiful. And some men loved her mind. Her boss certainly did at first, but she had not been interested in that. But Robert. He had been the perfect bachelor. Why had he chosen her? Were these things enough for him?

His hand found hers and slowly caressed it. "You'll do great today. I know you will."

"I hope so," she said and wished it were as easy as that. What would he do if she lost? Would he still love her in failure?

She pushed those thoughts away. She would not fail. She could not fail. She could not let that woman, Sarah Breme, down. Sarah, who seemed as meek as a ten year old girl. Sarah, who had concern and fear in her eyes every time they pored over the details of the case looking for some clue that would vindicate her story. That little woman did not seem capable of killing her husband, of stabbing him repeatedly in the back with a knife. Rachel believed she was innocent, just as she believed Robert loved her, and would love her irrespective of her success or failure. It was just something she felt inside.

Buoyed on love, she moved to her brightly lit, sparsely but tastefully decorated study room and picked up her defense brief—and lost her feeling of buoyancy.

This case would make or break her and she saw no way of winning with what she had now.

She had lost her previous three cases.

"Win this one or you are out," her boss, Mr. Fogworth of Hiswell and Fogworth Law Agency, had stated flatly. It seemed to her that Mr. Fogworth had taken a dislike to her and that was why she had been saddled with this tough case.

Her client, Sarah Breme, would be facing a first degree murder charge in the court the next day. She was being tried for the murder of her husband, Robert Breme. The prosecution had rested their case. It was now all up to Rachel.

Based on Sarah's file and her various interviews with Sarah, she was forced to admit that all the facts of the case were totally against her client. The prosecution had not even offered her a plea bargain.

Sarah's husband had been stabbed in his sitting room. It was established in the court that she had been the only person present in the room with her husband at the time of his death. Their next door neighbor, a Mr. Hamilton Miller, had heard her scream and had come running to find her standing over her husband's body holding the murder weapon —a bloodied knife—in her hand. Mr. Miller had called the police who had subsequently arrested Sarah for the murder of her husband.

As Rachel reviewed the facts, she found no way to get her client off. And yet, she was certain of her client's innocence. Sarah said she did not do it, and Rachel believed her. She just felt Sarah was telling the truth. A feeling would not get Sarah off though.

Rachel was frustrated. She looked out of her window into the night. The window of her room overlooked a fenced and beautifully cultivated lawn which was now illuminated by the street light. The weather outside was pleasant, but it made no impression on Rachel. She could not enjoy the weather with this case on her mind.

Rachel re-read the notes she had made of her last interview with Sarah, the day before for the hundredth time.

As she read, her mind supplied the background.

Ahmed A. Khan

When Sarah, in her rumpled and creased prison uniform, was brought into the interview room under police escort, she had looked miserable and confused. Rachel's heart had gone out to her.

"Did you kill your husband?" Rachel asked.

"No," she said adamantly.

"Then why was the murder weapon in your hands?"

"I heard angry words being exchanged between my husband and our neighbor, Mr Miller in the sitting room. Then I heard my husband scream. I came in and saw my husband lying with a knife in his back. I pulled it out to see if I could do anything to save him." Sarah said. "I knew my nurse's training could help. If his wound wasn't serious, I could save him."

"Weren't you afraid that touching the murder weapon would implicate you?"

"No."

"Why not?"

"Because I never thought that anyone would doubt the truth of my words."

Was Sarah really that naïve?

"It has been established that there was no one in the house at the time of murder except you and your husband. Mr. Miller has testified under oath that he entered your house only when he heard your husband's scream. What do you have to say to that?"

"He is lying," Sarah said with conviction.

"Why would he do that?"

"Because he killed my husband."

Rachel's heart sank. They were going in circles. Even if Sarah was telling the truth—and somehow, against the evidence, Rachel believed that she was—there was no way she could prove it before the court. She was going to lose this case and lose her job. More importantly, she would not be able to save poor Sarah.

"Do you have any proof of what you say?" She continued in spite of her sense of futility.

"Isn't my word good enough?"

"Why would Mr. Miller kill your husband? You said angry words were exchanged between them. What were they fighting about?"

"Mr. Miller tried to seduce me. I told my husband and when Mr. Miller came to visit, my husband confronted him about it. Mr. Miller

must have been carrying a knife with him."

"Only your finger prints were found on the knife and not Mr. Millers. Why?"

"Mr. Miller's hands were disfigured in an accident, so he wears gloves all of the time."

Prisons depressed Rachel. She had left as soon as she could.

Rachel closed the transcript, sat back in her chair and closed her eyes. What was it about the testimony that disturbed her?

Rachel, in several meetings with Sarah, had found that she was an unusual woman—open, honest, considerate, friendly and calm even as she faced the murder charge. She still could not imagine Sarah hurting anyone, let alone murdering her husband. Rachel wondered at her conviction of Sarah's innocence. What made her so sure? Her feelings were always based on facts, even if she unconsciously recognized them. What was she recognizing now? If only she could find it.

Isn't my word good enough?

Sarah's words rang in her ears. What a strange statement! Words were never good enough. She needed evidence. Then why did Sarah think people should believe her solely on her words? She opened her eyes and sat up straight. She sat motionless for several minutes, thinking, thinking.

The next morning at half past nine, Rachel parked her blue Honda Accord in its designated place at the parking lot and made her way to the courthouse, carefully avoiding protestors. One of them recognized her as a lawyer and nearly hit her with his sign. She pushed the "Ban Androids!" sign away just as the police came rushing in.

"People aren't meant to be perfect!" the protester shouted as he was dragged away. "Only angels are supposed to be perfect! Only Jesus!"

I wish people could be more like androids. Totally sane, totally considerate, and operating under Asimov's laws.

It was a bright summer day and the old stone building of the court house, squat and vast, sprawled in the sunlight like an anachronism amidst the modern utilitarian and high rise architecture laced with sky walks and sky rails.

The courthouse was an anachronism in more than one way. It was one of the very few institutions that carried its business in the cyber age as it had done in the last few centuries.

The courtroom was almost full. The trial seemed to have gained

Ahmed A. Khan

quite a lot of publicity. Ghouls. That was all these people were. She knew that most of the spectators were convinced of Sarah's guilt and were following the case to see if the jury would award her the death penalty. *They are in for a surprise, if I can help it.*

Rachel drew several appreciative glances from the male population of the courtroom. Was that all men truly saw? Her looks? She resisted the urge to adjust her business skirt and instead pushed back a loose strand of wheat colored hair.

At twenty four, Rachel Roquefort was one of the youngest and one of the better known legal counsels in the country. As an intern two years ago, she had made a name for herself in the famous "Robots" case. Though the major part of the work was done by her senior, Mr. Hiswell, her successful appellate argument played its part in making the testimony of robots and androids admissible in the country's judiciary system. That is why she was accosted by protesters like the man in the parking lot. They hated her for siding with the man-made angels, as they called them, and the men who made them.

Prosecutor Julian Hemple was at his place and looked up when Rachel entered. He smiled at her smugly, sure of his victory. Rachel sweetly smiled back at him.

"What's she got to smile about?" whispered young William Bagford, Hemple's assistant.

Julian shrugged.

"You think she's going to pull a rabbit out of her hat?"

"Fat chance," said Hemple. "You are reading too many of those ancient Perry Mason courtroom thrillers."

All the people related to the case were present in the court. Sarah's neighbor, Hamilton Miller, was there and so was his wife. The police constable who had arrested Sarah was there. But Rachel had eyes only for Sarah.

Sarah Breme was in her place. She smiled at Rachel as Rachel sat down beside her. Rachel whispered a question.

Sarah's mouth dropped open. "How did you know?"

It was now Rachel's turn to be stunned. Her wild hunch had turned out to be true. Her mind raced through the steps she must take. She was still not sure of her success. Her one consolation was that Judge Jonas Mott was an intelligent and reasonable man.

"Why didn't you tell me before now?" Rachel was furious. It would have saved so much time and anguish.

"I promised my husband never to reveal his secret."

Just then everybody stood up as Judge Mott entered the court and took his seat. He was followed by the traditional twelve jurors, six men and six women from different age groups and different social and professional backgrounds.

"Court is now in session," Judge Mott declared.

Rachel rose from her seat. "Your Honor, if it pleases the court, the defense requests a continuation."

"Objection," snapped Julian.

The judge looked first at Rachel and then at Julian.

"Would both counsels approach the bench?"

Rachel and Julian approached the bench.

"Why does the defense require extra time?"

"Some new developments have come up, your honor, which make it imperative for us to have some extra time."

"That's all nonsense, and the defense knows it too," snorted Julian. "This is just an unnecessary delaying tactic on the part of the defense."

"The prosecuting counsel has no right to measure everyone by his own standards," she said, smiling sweetly.

"I do not tolerate personal attacks in my court," Judge Mott's tone was firm. Then he turned to Rachel.

"How much time do you require?"

"Just two hours, Your Honor."

"The court sees no problem in acceding to this request. The court will recess for two hours and will recommence at noon." He gathered his robes and gracefully swept out of the courtroom.

Prosecutor Julian Hemple was forty five, tall and quite distinguished despite his receding hairline.

Hemple firmly believed in the guilt of Sarah Breme. He would believe in the guilt of any wife implicated in the murder of her husband. Two years back, Julian Hemple had lost his faith in women. It was then that his wife had left him for a multi-millionaire businessman. And she had taken their only daughter with her.

This case was particularly important to him because it involved not one, but two women: Sarah Breme and her attorney, Rachel Roquefort. By having a guilty verdict brought against Sarah Breme, he would be getting back at two women with one fell swoop.

He could already taste victory on his tongue. It was a sweet taste. And soon it would be fully his. This was an open and shut case. So he waited impatiently.

At noon, the court recommenced. Rachel waived her opening statement.

"As our first and only witness," she declared, "I call Dr. James Merritt to the witness stand."

"Who is this James Merritt and where does he come into the case?" Julian Hemple whispered to William Bagford.

"I don't know."

"Find out fast."

"You think this is the rabbit?"

"Just go." William Bagford left the court.

"Objection," roared Hemple. "This witness has not been disclosed by the counsel."

Rachel calmly flipped a Westlaw printout onto the prosecutor's table. She then approached the bench and handed a copy to the judge.

"Judge," she said, "in the case of Bartell vs. McMurty, decided last year, the federal 9th circuit held that in special circumstances defendants can introduce undisclosed witnesses."

The judge skimmed the printout, running a long finger over its words, occasionally nodding.

"Counsel," he said to the prosecutor, "Ms. Roquefort appears to be correct on that point. I am going to allow the witness unless you think the cited decision can be distinguished somehow from the facts in this case."

"Your honor, I am aware of the precedent, but it is our position that it does not apply here as there are no special circumstances in this case."

"Your honor, I undertake to prove the special circumstances through the testimony of this witness."

"Objection overruled. Proceed with your witness."

Dr. Merritt took the stand. In his right hand he carried a small camera-like gadget.

"Dr. Merritt, would you please tell the court about your field of expertise?" Rachel began.

"I am a robotics engineer."

"Would you please elaborate on that?"

"I build robots and androids."

"And you are an expert in the field?"

"My peers think so."

"What is that gadget that you have in your hand?"

"This is called an android identifier."

"What do you use it for?"

"Objection, your honor," said Julian Hemple. "This line of questioning is irrelevant to the case."

The Judge looked at Rachel. "I think the prosecuting counsel is right. Unless you can give some good reason for this line of questioning, I will sustain the objection."

"Your honor, if you please, I will show the relevance within a few minutes."

"Under that stipulation, I will allow you to continue with your questioning."

"Thank you, your honor." She turned to Dr. Merritt. "As I was asking, Dr. Merritt, what do you use your gadget for?"

"I use it to test a person to find out if they are an android or a normal human being."

"How does it work?"

"As you probably know, all androids have identity microchips embedded in their foreheads. No android can function without these microchips. This gadget detects the presence of the microchips, and records the data found on them."

"What necessitated the designing of such gadgets?"

"It is against the law, but sometimes androids pose as human beings."

"Do all androids have the identify microchip embedded in their foreheads?"

"Yes."

"Why?"

"With the development of tissue culture and DNA technology and with its use in robotics, it became possible to design robots that could pass for human beings in any physical or psychological test. These chips were designed so that the androids could be distinguished from human beings."

"Is it possible for an android to remove this microchip in order to

Ahmed A. Khan

avoid identification?"

"No. The androids are designed such that with the removal of the microchip all their bodily functions would cease and they would be dead in effect."

Rachel could have cut her questions short. At this point she was asking questions that would be asked by the prosecutor in his cross examination. But she was fully intent not to leave the prosecution any ground for cross examination.

She continued. "Suppose a human being gets this chip embedded in his or her forehead. Can he or she get away posing as an android?"

"Not with this gadget, no." Dr. Merritt patted the machine affectionately. "There is a setting on this gadget that would render an android immobile. I would think it would be very difficult for a human being to fake total immobility for any length of time. Then there are several other considerations, too. How would a person know when to fake immobility if I were to select the immobility settings surreptitiously?"

"In short, you, as an expert in your field, state that if you use this gadget you can conclusively and irrefutably identify an android from a human being?"

"Yes. I would stake my reputation on it."

"Did you recently test anyone with that gadget?"

"Yes."

"When was this?"

"An hour ago."

"Who was present at the time of testing beside yourself and the person who was being tested?"

"The chief of police and two constables were present at the time of testing."

"And what did you find?"

"I found that the person I tested was indeed an android posing as a human being."

"Do you see that person in this courtroom?"

"Yes."

"Who is it?"

Dr. Merritt raised his hand and pointed. "It is the defendant, Sarah Breme. She is an android."

Pandemonium. Julian Hemple's face went pale. He knew he was beaten. He thought of putting up a show of cross examination but gave the idea up as futile.

Another person whose face changed color was Hamilton Miller, Sarah's neighbor. If it had been an earlier century, Miller would have tried to bolt, but in this age of electronic currency, there was no way he could live without using his credit card or his ID, and if he did, that would be his last free moment. Escape was futile. He accepted the inevitable and waited.

After the dust settled down, the jury returned with a verdict of not guilty for Sarah Breme, admonishing her for her masquerade. She would face penalties, but nothing as severe as death.

Judge Jonas Mott summed up the case. "After establishing beyond doubt that the defendant Sarah Breme is actually an android, the court accepts her testimony as the whole truth. In view of her testimony, she is declared not guilty. On the other hand, the court instructs the Prosecutor's office to have Mr. Hamilton Miller arrested and tried for the murder of Mr. Robert Breme." The judge paused. "And Sarah Breme is instructed never to masquerade as a human being in future."

Rachel had triumphed. Sarah was free. But she was not free to masquerade as a human again. Gone were her days of living *that* kind of freedom.

Sarah leaned over to Rachel. "I am not sure if I want to thank you. I will miss living like a human. And I will miss his touch, how much he needed me and wanted me close." Sarah stood and walked away.

Robert was waiting for her outside, a dashing smile on his face. "You were brilliant. Just brilliant. We need to celebrate. You pick the restaurant." He twined his perfect fingers in hers and led her away.

As they walked away, Rachel fingered her purse and the odd bulge that was Dr. Merritt's android identifier. Should she use it?

Ahmed A. Khan